英汉对照典藏本

英语文学开山之作
盎格鲁－撒克逊民族史诗

# 贝奥武甫

[英] 佚 名 著

陈才宇 译

浙江工商大学出版社

·杭州·

**图书在版编目(CIP)数据**

贝奥武甫：英、汉 / (英)佚名著；陈才宇译. —杭州：
浙江工商大学出版社，2021.1
ISBN 978-7-5178-4161-6

Ⅰ.①贝… Ⅱ.①佚… ②约… ③陈… Ⅲ.①史诗—
英国—古代—英、汉 Ⅳ.①I561.22

中国版本图书馆 CIP 数据核字(2020)第 218535 号

# 贝奥武甫
**BEIAOWUFU**

[英]佚 名 著

陈才宇 译

出 品 人　鲍观明
责任编辑　沈　娴
责任校对　王黎明
封面设计　观止堂 _ 未氓
插　　图　郑思佳
责任印制　包建辉
出版发行　浙江工商大学出版社
　　　　　(杭州市教工路 198 号　邮政编码 310012)
　　　　　(E-mail：zjgsupress@163.com)
　　　　　(网址：http://www.zjgsupress.com)
　　　　　电话：0571-88904980，88831806(传真)
排　　版　杭州朝曦图文设计有限公司
印　　刷　浙江海虹彩色印务有限公司
开　　本　880mm×1230mm　1/32
印　　张　8.875
字　　数　183 千
版 印 次　2021 年 1 月第 1 版　2021 年 1 月第 1 次印刷
书　　号　ISBN 978-7-5178-4161-6
定　　价　66.00 元

# CONTENTS/目录

完整。

　　浙江工商大学出版社此次以双语的形式出版这部史诗，并将它与拙译《高文爵士与绿衣骑士》《罗宾汉》《浮士德博士的悲剧》合辑成一个系列。这样的出版是很有意义的。所收的诗歌和诗剧虽不能说全面反映了英国早期叙事诗歌的情况，但都有代表性。由于是双语本，也方便读者对照着查验我的译文。译得不妥甚至译错的地方，还望贤明之士赐教之。

**陈才宇**

2019年3月15日于杭州寓所

史诗第一部分写主人公的青年时代,第二部分写他的老年时期,这是结构的对衬。主要情节的童话性质和插曲的现实性,这是内容的虚实对衬。另外,作为武士的贝奥武甫和狂妄的武士安佛斯,以及作为国王的贝奥武甫和暴虐无道的海勒摩德,则构成人物形象的对衬。

如果说对衬法的作用主要是用来深化主题,加强人物的形象性,那么,暗示法所起的则是心理影响的作用,以先兆性为特征。这一手法在《贝奥武甫》中运用得很普遍。如贝奥武甫杀死魔怪格兰道尔以后,丹麦歌手在庆功会上唱了西格蒙德屠龙的故事,这里暗示了贝奥武甫后来与毒龙交战的事。史诗一开头描写丹麦国王赫罗斯加的祖先希尔德的葬礼,这里暗示着贝奥武甫与毒龙同归于尽后高特人为他举行的葬礼。有趣的是,希尔德的儿子叫贝奥,这是历史的巧合呢,还是作者有意的安排?笔者认为后者的可能性大。当然,从艺术的角度看,这种为暗示而暗示的手法未必高明,因为一般的读者更欣赏的是情节有机结合的作品。

我的翻译主要依据 *Anglo-Saxon Books: Beowulf* (Middlesex, 1991),这是一个古英语与现代英语的逐字对照本,现代英语译者是约翰·波特(John Porter)。这个本子的好处是译文与原文之间实行了语言信息的对等,不足之处是文法差异所造成的对现代英语文本可读性的损害。为了解决这个矛盾,我便同时参考了 *The Anglo-Saxon World* (Kevin Crossley-Holland, Oxford University Press, 1982)中的现代英语译本和 *Norton Anthology of English Literature* (4th ed.)中的散文改写本。尤其是后者,对我的帮助很大。史诗原文押头韵。这种韵式在汉语中是没有的,我只能将遗憾留在译文中。尝试弥补时,也只能用尾韵随机凑合。还有,古英语原文中,每一诗行通常有两顿。我一般用意群转述之。实在得不到两个意群时,宁可牺牲形式而保全意义的的老人,但为了王国和人民的利益,还是义无反顾地承担了最大的风险。毒龙被杀死后,他受了致命伤,临终前仍念念不忘自己的子民。如此无私无畏、爱民如子的国王,必然受到百姓的爱戴和拥护。

总之,贝奥武甫这个人物,既是臣僚阶层的楷模,又是理想的国王。史诗中有关他的双重角色的描写,反映了盎格鲁-撒克逊人对这两种社会角色的道德规范的期许与憧憬。

在艺术方面,史诗《贝奥武甫》也很有特色。首先是"插曲"的多彩多姿,充分体现了整理者对叙述手法的把握。关于赫纳夫与芬恩之间血腥屠杀的故事,安插在贝奥武甫杀死格兰道尔以后。丹麦国王赫罗斯加为了给贝奥武甫庆功,在宴会厅举行盛大宴会,民间歌手演唱了这支悲歌。丹麦国王嫁女以调解血仇未果的故事是在贝奥武甫回高特王国以后由他自己向海格拉克叙述海外历险时提到的。当时最后的结局尚未出现,据贝奥武甫"推测",这种以联姻换取的和约很快就将维持不下去。与贝奥武甫直接有关的那段"插曲",即奥尼拉追杀其侄儿导致赫德莱德搭上性命的故事,则是通过史诗作者自己的口吻说出的。其他几个小"插曲"的表现形式也不同:赫罗斯加与女婿间的自相残杀采用的是提前交代的方式;安佛斯杀害自己的亲兄弟一事则通过对话予以揭示。叙述手段的多样性使史诗的结构显得灵活多变、跌宕起伏。

不过,有必要指出:史诗所运用的这种"插曲"艺术尽管具有富于变化的优点,但并不是很完美。最大的缺陷是与主要情节的衔接不够自然、流畅,容易产生突兀感。难怪有的批评家会指责史诗的结构与情节太杂乱纷繁,像一个破布袋子,里面塞满了北欧各民族的历史片断,使人看得眼花缭乱。

《贝奥武甫》另外两个重要的艺术特点是运用对衬法和暗示法。

吻合。

这里就有一个问题:史诗的作者,那些盎格鲁-撒克逊人,为什么要借托历史人物敷演出一个非现实的半神半人的形象呢?

简单地用古民造神的动机去解释,恐怕难以令人信服。贝奥武甫虽然被史诗的作者加以神化,但毕竟还不是一个真正的神。他的活动空间在人间,而不是在一个超自然的环境里。盎格鲁-撒克逊人之所以要虚构贝奥武甫这个英雄形象,是想在他身上寄托他们的美好理想与追求。他们通过贝奥武甫不仅宣扬了他们的宗教观和神话意识,更重要的是,传达了他们的世界观和他们关于伦理道德的基本知识。

史诗的第一部分写主人公的青年时代。丹麦王国受到魔怪骚扰,生灵涂炭,贝奥武甫得到消息后毅然前往救援。这行为本身表明他不仅具有见义勇为的侠士精神,而且具有国家间和民族间睦邻友好的思想。当时的欧洲社会,王国与王国之间,氏族与氏族之间的斗争极其残酷,能长期和平共处的相邻王国寥寥无几。贝奥武甫能为别国人民的利益挺身而出,从个人动机而言,固然看重自身的名誉,但这种对于名誉的追求是有益于氏族间和平的。在丹麦王宫,他并不因自己的勇武而妄自尊大,而是虚怀若谷,彬彬有礼,始终恪守臣子之礼。在自己人面前,他恭顺得像一头羔羊;但一旦走上战场,面对敌人,又凶猛得像一头狮子。这种对友恭顺、对敌勇敢的精神后来被骑士文学反复颂扬。从这个意义上说,贝奥武甫不仅是盎格鲁-撒克逊人心目中一个理想的英雄,而且是英国文学史上第一位道德完美的骑士。

贝奥武甫后来成了国王,但他的王位也不是刻意图谋来的。老国王阵亡后,王后欲立他为高特国王,他不受,甘愿辅佐王子赫德莱德。直到赫德莱德去世后,他才登基为王。这一行动足以表明他具有坦荡的胸怀和忠诚无私的品格。国内出现毒龙为害的事件时,他已是年迈武士贝奥武甫率十四勇士前往救援。经过激烈的搏斗,力大无穷的贝奥武甫扯断魔怪的一条胳膊。垂死的魔怪逃回洞穴。次日晚上,格兰道尔之母前来为她的儿子报仇。贝奥武甫与她在水潭下展开殊死搏斗,最后用魔剑将她杀死。

第二部分(1904—3182行)写贝奥武甫屠龙。故事的主人公此时已继承大位,成功地统治高特王国长达五十年。就在壮士暮年,国内出现一条毒龙。此龙因自己守护的财宝被盗,向高特人报复。它口吐烈焰,烧毁村庄,荼毒生灵。为了拯救自己的王国和人民,贝奥武甫毅然进入龙窟。在一位名叫威格拉夫的年轻武士的援助下,将毒龙杀死,但老英雄也因受伤过重,献出了自己的生命。

从情节看,《贝奥武甫》具有民间童话性质:主人公三战妖魔,就是民间童话的典型结构。吃人的巨人、吐火的毒龙,都是民间童话中反复出现的母题。按照民间故事类型学分析,贝奥武甫战格兰道尔,属于降妖型的故事;杀毒龙则是开洞取宝型故事的演变。史诗的作者将这两种类型的故事合并起来,塑造出贝奥武甫的英雄形象。这个例子告诉我们:民间童话的题材是可以写成史诗的。

民间童话大多是虚拟的。承认《贝奥武甫》具有童话性,即意味着承认它的内容的非现实性。但据有关学者考证,历史上确实有过贝奥武甫这个人,而且确实是史诗中提到的高特国王海格拉克的外甥。有一次,海格拉克率舰队劫掠莱茵河下游弗里西亚人的土地,当时该地是法兰克王国的一部分。他们获得赃物甚丰,正欲启程回去,忽遭法兰克士兵的袭击。海格拉克死于战场。贝奥武甫杀死一名法兰克旗手,泅水逃回高特。这件事约发生于公元521年,史诗《贝奥武甫》中穿插提到过四次,正好与6世纪法兰克都尔教会主教、史学家格雷戈里(Grégoire)的《法兰克人史》和无名氏的《法兰克史记》所记载的史实

# 译　序

　　史诗《贝奥武甫》是古英语文学中最重要的一首叙事诗,代表着英国古代文学的最高成就。早在六七世纪,它就以口头形式流传于日耳曼民族聚居的北欧沿海。盎格鲁-撒克逊人入侵不列颠以后,它随着征服者的足迹来到新的居住地开花结实。如果说英国民族是一个"舶来的民族",那么,《贝奥武甫》就是一部"舶来的史诗"。

　　今天我们读到的本子是公元1000年左右用西撒克逊语整理的。这时候的不列颠与三百多年前已大不一样:以异教思想为主导的氏族制度已经解体,取而代之的是封建土地所有制。基督教经历了从圣·奥古斯丁初期传播到取得英国国教地位的全过程,教会的势力发展到与封建贵族分享国家政权的地步。作为上层建筑的文化教育控制在教士手中。《贝奥武甫》在这个时候形成定本,必然烙上时代的印记。史诗的整理者是谁,已无法稽考,但肯定是一位教士。他在记录民间流传的故事时将一些基督教的观念添加进去,从而使作品所体现的信仰观念具有两重性,即多神教和一神教这两种思想交织在一起,比如反复无常的命运之神就常常与仁慈的上帝同日而语。反映在宗教观念上的这种交错糅合,应引起研究者的重视。

　　史诗的基本情节可分两部分。第一部分(1—1903行)写贝奥武甫剪除魔怪:丹麦国王赫罗斯加兴建了一座宏伟的宴会厅,遭到魔怪格兰道尔的袭击。魔怪为所欲为,为害丹麦王国长达十二年之久。高特

1

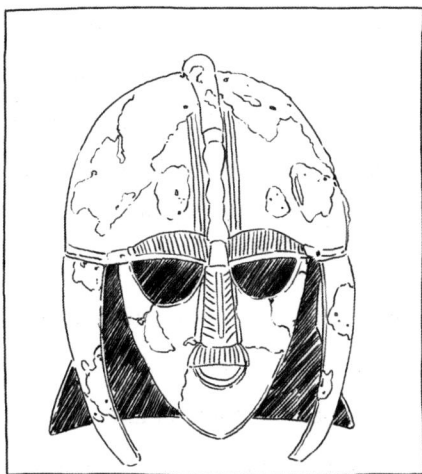

Sutton Hoo Helmet

萨顿胡头盔

（盎格鲁-撒克逊头盔，出土于英国萨福克
郡萨顿胡船葬，600—650）

# PROLOGUE
## The Earlier History of the Danes

What! We Spear-Danes'    in yore-days,
tribe-kings'    glory heard,
how the leaders    courage accomplished.
Often Scyld, Scef's son,    from enemies' bands,
5    from many tribes    mead-benches seized,
terrorized earls,    since first he was
destitute found;    he its relief knew,
grew under skies,    in honours throve,
until to him each    neighbour
10    over whale-road    submit must,
tribute yield;    that was good king!
To him heir was    after born
young in dwellings,    him God sent
to folk for solace;    intense misery saw
15    that they before felt,    leaderless
a long while;    him for it Life-Lord,
glory's Ruler,    world-honour gave,
Beow was famed,    renown widely sprang
of Scyld's heir    Danish lands in.
20    So shall young man    by good deeds ensure,

# 引　子
## 丹麦早期的历史

诸位安静! 我们已经听说,

在遥远的过去,丹麦的王公、首领,

如何将英雄的业绩一一创建。

斯基夫之子希尔德,常常从敌人手中,

5　从诸多部落那里,夺得领土,

想当初他孤苦伶仃,如今却

威震四方酋长;他已如愿以偿,

在天地间建功立业,声誉日增,

鲸鱼之路四邻的部落

10　不得不逐一向他臣服,

向他纳贡;哦,好强大的国王!

不久以后,在他的王宫

降生了一位王子,那是上帝

给人民带来的安慰:他曾目睹

15　久无首领的黎民百姓饱受痛苦,

生命的主宰,光荣的统帅

因此赐予他世上的荣耀。

贝奥声名卓著,希尔德之子的功勋

在北部地区被人到处颂扬。

20　年轻的王子侍奉在父王左右,

by fine fee-gifts    while in father's care,

that him in age    again stand by

choice-companions    when war comes,

men support him;    by praise-deeds shall

25    in tribe every,    man prosper.

Then Scyld departed    at destined time

full-strong to fare    in Lord's keeping;

they him then carried    to briny's current

precious companions,    as he himself bade

30    when words wielded    friend of Scyldings,

loved land-ruler    long reigned.

There at harbour stood    ringed-prow

icy and out-keen,    hero's vessel;

they laid down then    loved chieftain,

35    rings' bestower,    in bosom of ship,

mighty by mast.    There were treasures many

from far-ways    fortunes brought;

not heard I comelier    keel arrayed

with battle-wea pons    and war-clothes,

40    with blades and byrnies;    him on bosom lay

treasures many    which with him should

in flood's hold    far off travel.

In no way they him less    with gifts endowed,

with folk-wealth,    than those did

45    who him at outset    forth sent

他应该品行端正,赏赐大方,

以便将来有忠诚的伙伴

追随在身边,一旦发生战争,

他们将为他效命;不管是谁,

25　要想建功立业,首先得受人称赞。

但时限一到,希尔德一命归天,

这位勇士回到了主的身边。

遵照他的嘱咐,亲密的伙伴们

把他抬到海边,这位丹麦人的朋友,

30　可敬的国王,曾经发号施令,

长久地治理过这个国家。

港口停泊着国王的灵船,

船身结着一层冰,正准备起航;

他们将可敬的首领抬进船舱,

35　就这样,这位项圈的赐予者

充满荣耀地靠近桅杆。他的身边

堆着来自四方的无数财宝;

我从未听说世上有哪艘航船

曾装载过那么多的武器和甲胄,

40　那么多的战刀和锁子甲;他的胸前

还摆满金子银子,它们将随着他

一道远远地漂流,进入大海的怀抱。

他们把礼物慷慨地送给国王,

那都是人民的财物,想当初,

45　襁褓中他独自漂洋过海,带来一船财宝,

alone over waves      infant-being.

Then yet they set up      standard golden

high over head,      they let sea carry,

gave to ocean;      in them was gloomy heart,

50    mourning mind.      Men not can

say for truth,      hall-counsellors,

heroes under heaven,      who that cargo received.


Then was in burghs      Beow the Scylding

loved people-king      a long age

55    among folk famed      —father elsewhere went,

elder from earth—      until to him in turn was born

high Halfdane;      ruled while he lived,

old and war-fierce,      glad Scyldings.

To him four bairns      forth-counted

60    in world were born,      armies' leader,

Heorogar and Hrothgar      and Halga good,

heard I that Yrse      was Onela's queen,

the Battle-Scylfing's      bed-companion.

这次他带走的礼品绝不比那次少。
在他头顶,他们还竖起一面锦旗,
然后让海水把他卷进海洋。
他们的内心是何等的悲伤!

50　无论宫廷的智者还是天下的英雄,
没有人能够确切地知道
这一船货物最后到了谁的手中。


从此以后,贝奥成了可敬的丹麦国王,
治理一座城堡,在黎民百姓中
55　长久地享有盛誉,(他的父王已经去世,
告别了自己的家园,)直到后来,
贝奥又生下伟大的哈夫丹,
他一生驰骋疆场,庇护希尔德的子孙。
他们都说他生有三子一女:
60　军事统帅希罗加和赫罗斯加,
好人儿哈尔格,我还听说
公主伊丝成了奥尼拉的王后,
那位骁勇的瑞典人的伴侣。

# PART ONE

## The Hall Is Attacked by Grendel

Then was to Hrothgar     war-luck given,

65 battle's honour,     so that him his retainers

keenly kept by     until the young war-band grew

retinue mighty.     Him in mind ran

that hall-house     command he would

mead-room mightier     men to build

70 than human sons     ever heard of,

and there within     all deal out

to young and old     such as him God gave,

except folk-land     and lives of men.

Then I widely heard     work ordered

75 from many a tribe     through this middle-earth,

folk-hall to furnish.     For him in time it came,

quick among men,     that it was all-ready,

of hall-rooms' hugest;     gave it Heorot name

he who his word's wield     widely had.

80 He boast not belied,     rings dealt out,

treasure at feast.     Hall towered

high and horn-gabled;     war-surges it awaited

of loathed fire;     nor was it for long yet

# 一
## 格兰道尔袭击鹿厅

赫罗斯加战场上捷报频传，

65 荣耀无比，手下人无不心甘情愿

追随在他身边，他麾下的人马

一天天壮大。他于是心中策划

建造一座宴乐大厅，宏大的规模

要让他们的子孙后代闻所未闻，

70 在那里，他可以向部下颁发战利品，

他要将上帝赐予他的一切，

除了公地和人的生命，

都奖赏给手下的老将和新兵。

我听说动工的命令下达到四面八方，

75 众多部落应命而来，大家齐心协力

共建这座人厅。不久以后，

大厦按时落成，一如人们期望，

拔地而起的是一座宏大的殿堂；

号令天下的国王给大厦起名"鹿厅"。①  ① 鹿象征王权。

80 他遵守诺言，宴席中分赐

戒指和珠宝。大厦耸立，

山墙雄伟壮观；它在等待

仇恨的烈火将它付之一炬；

9

that the sword-hate      of oath-swearers

85   after deadly feud      awaken should.

   Then the fierce beast      terribly

time endured,      he who in darkness dwelt,

that he day every      rejoicing heard

loud in hall;      there was harp's clang,

90   clear song of poet.      Spoke he who could

origin of men      far back reckon,

said that the Almighty      earth wrought,

fair bright field      which water surrounds,

set up triumphant      sun and moon,

95   lustre as light      for land-dwellers,

and adorned      earth's regions

with limbs and leaves;      life too He shaped

for species each      which living moves.

   So the lord's men      in joys lived,

100   happily,      until one began

evil to inflict,      fiend in hell;

was the ghastly spirit      Grendel called,

noted march-stepper,      he who moors held,

fen and fastness;      fiend-kin's land

105   wretched creature      ruled a while,

since him Creator      condemned had

in Cain's kin—      the killing avenged

eternal Lord      in which he Abel slew;

如今还不到时候,翁婿间那场血仇

85　尚未爆发,血腥的屠杀只是后话。①

却说当时有个可怕的恶魔,

他安营扎寨在黑暗的地方,

每天他都听见大厅里欢声笑语,

竖琴弹奏,吟游诗人放开歌喉,

90　这使他难以忍受,因为诗人歌唱

遥远的过去,人类的起源,

万能的主如何创造大地,

让田野充满阳光,周围出现海洋;

如何胜利地创造出太阳与月亮,

95　让它们以明澈的光辉照耀人寰;

如何用树木和绿叶装点世界;

如何创造出各种各样的生命,

让其能够生活,能够呼吸。

就这样,国王的战士欢欢喜喜

100　生活在鹿厅,直到地狱的魔鬼

前来作恶,向他们滋事寻衅;

这恶魔的名字叫作格兰道尔,

他是塞外的漫游者,占据着

荒野与沼泽;这可恶的怪物

105　统治着一片鬼魅出没的土地,

那里是该隐子孙的庇护所,

自从该隐残杀了自己的兄弟亚伯,

永恒的主就严惩了他的后裔。

① 为了避免仇杀,赫罗斯加将女儿嫁给敌国,但战争仍未能避免。鹿厅后来被大火烧毁。

11

not enjoyed He the feud,     but He him far drove out,

110     Ruler, for the crime,     mankind from.

Thence un-things     all arose,

ogres and elves     and monsters,

also giants,     who with God fought

a long time;     he them its reward paid.


115     Went then to find,     when night came,

high house,     how it Ring-Danes

after beer-feast     furnished had.

Found then therein     nobles' band

sleeping after feast;     sorrow not they knew,

120     misery of men.     Thing of malice,

grim and greedy,     ready soon was,

fierce and furious,     and from rest seized

thirty thanes;     thence back went

in plunder proud     to hom faring,

125     with the death-feast     dwelling to seek.

Then was at dawning     with early day

Grendel's war-strength     to men un-secret.

Then was after feast     lament up raised,

great morning-cry.     Mighty chieftain,

130     noble king old-good,     unhappy sat,

suffered severely,     thane-sorrow endured,

when they the foe's     footprints scanned,

主厌恶这样的仇杀，由于这桩罪恶，

110  主把他驱逐到荒无人烟的边鄙。

从此，那里滋生了大批妖孽，

其中有食人魔、精灵、怪物，

还有巨人，他们长期与上帝抗争，

上帝给了他们应有的报应。


115  夜幕降临，这恶魔来到大厅，

探察佩戴金环的丹麦人

如何在这里举行盛大的欢宴。

他发现高贵的武士已经酒足饭饱，

一个个进入梦乡；他们全然不知

120  悲伤与痛苦即将来临；这恶魔

既凶狠又贪婪，他急不可待，

即刻伸出野蛮而残忍的魔爪，

抓起其中三十个酣睡的战士，

然后得意扬扬，带着战利品

125  返回他所居住的老巢。

第二天一早，破晓的天光下，

格兰道尔的暴行赫然在目，

欢宴后迎来悲伤，清晨的号哭。

高贵的国王闷闷不乐地坐着，

130  内心极其痛苦；当他看见

那该诅咒的仇敌留下的足迹，

他为自己的人民深感悲痛；

cursed spirit's;    was the strife too strong,

loathed and lengthy.    Not was it longer time,

135    but after one night    again he caused

murder-death more,    and not mourned for it,

feud and felony;    he was too fixed on them.

Then was easy-found    he who him elsewhere

further off    rest sought,

140    bed among bowers,    when to him shown was,

told truly    with clear token

hall-thane's hate;    held himself then

further and safer    he who the foe avoided.

Thus he ruled    and against right fought,

145    one against all.    until idle stood

house finest.    Was the while great;

twelve winters' time    trouble suffered

friend of Scyldings,    miseries all,

spacious sorrows;    and so to men became,

150    to human sons    clearly known

in songs sadly    that Grendel strove

a while with Hrothgar,    hate-spites waged,

felony and feud    for many seasons,

endless attack;    peace not he would

155    with men any    in army of Danes,

deadliness desist,    with fees atone;

not there any wise man    to hope needed

这场灾难实在太深重、太可恨!
然而,仅仅隔了一夜,那恶魔

135 毫无怜悯之心,再次进行了
血腥的屠杀;他早已一意孤行。
不难想见,希求安宁的人们
从此离开自己的家园,逃往别处,
在异域安家落户,因为有足够的证据

140 向他们表明,向他们明确显示
恶魔的仇恨占据了他们的鹿厅,
于是,那些幸免于难的人,
为了寻求安全,一个个远走高飞。
就这样,恶魔强占了鹿厅,以一敌众。

145 他与正义对抗,直到高高的大厦
变得空空荡荡。这段时间十分漫长;
整整十二个冬天,丹麦人的领袖
历尽困苦,蒙受万般的艰难、
无限的悲伤;这个不幸的故事

150 还被编成了歌谣,子孙后代无不知道
格兰道尔与赫罗斯加之间的争斗,
双方不共戴天,战争无休无止,
一直延续了许多个春秋;
恶魔不愿跟丹麦人和平相处,

155 不愿解怨消仇,或者赔偿损失。
明智的谋士,谁也不指望
凶手会为死者做出任何补偿。

for bright bounty     from slayer's hands,

but the monster     mauling was,

160    dark death-shadow,     veterans and youth;

he lurked and ambushed,     in endless night ruled

misty moors;     men not know

where hell-demons     in motions glide.

    Thus many offences     foe of mankind,

165    grim lone-walker,     often committed,

cruel crimes;     Heorot inhabited,

jewelled hall,     in black nights;

not he the gift-stool     to enjoy was able,

treasure get from Lord,     nor his favour know.

170     That was anguish great     for friend of Scyldings,

mind's breaking.     Many often sat,

keen men at counsel,     campaign discussed,

what for bold-hearts     best would be

against swift-horror     to adopt.

175    At times they pledged     in idol-shrines

sacred offerings,     in words prayed

that them soul-slayer     with aid would save

from people's-plight.     Such was habit their,

heathens' hope;     on hell they thought

180    in mind-heart,     Ruler they not recognised,

deeds' Deemer,     not knew they Lord God,

nor they yet heavens' Helm     to honour were able,

相反,这黑色的死亡之影

不断地攻击国王的新老士兵;

160　常常设下埋伏,伺机偷袭,

长夜中他统治着浓雾漫天的沼泽地,

没有人知道他究竟出没在哪里。

因此,这人类的死敌继续肆虐,

这可怕的独行者,人类的死敌

165　犯下的暴行,一件又一件,

每天晚上天一黑,他就侵犯

那座富丽堂皇的鹿厅;

只是他在那里得不到任何奖赏,

得不到主所赐予的财宝和恩惠。

170　丹麦人的贤王极其苦恼,

内心犹如刀绞。众多王公贵族

坐下商讨对策,献计谋划

如何派遣最坚强的武士

去抵御那令人生畏的侵犯。

175　他们还常常向异教的神灵

奉献牺牲,祈求那灵魂的屠宰者①　　　　① 指异教的神灵。

伸出援助之手把他们拯救,

使他们摆脱灾祸。对偶像抱着幻想

属于他们的陋习;他们心里

180　只想着地狱,不知有主宰者,

不知有仲裁者,不知有万能的主,

不知如何赞美天堂的保护者——

glory's Wielder.    Woe be to him who shall

through searing fear    soul shove

185    in fire's fathom,    relief not hope for,

naught to change!    Well be to him who may

after death-day    Lord seek out

and in Father's bosom    peace beseech!

# PART TWO

## The Coming of Beowulf to Heorot

So then in time-care    son of Halfdane

190    ceaseless seethed;    not could wise hero

woe turn away;    was the strife too harsh,

loathed and lengthy,    that on the people came,

throe-wrack torture-grim,    night-terror greatest.

That from home heard    Hygelac's thane

195    good among Geats,    Grendel's deeds;

he was of human    might strongest

in that day    of this life,

noble and prodigious.    He ordered him wave-crosser

那光荣的王。这是何等不幸啊!
陷于困境的人竟然让自己的灵魂

185　投入烈火的怀抱,受失望的煎熬,
而不思改弦更张! 这样的人有福了:
他们在死后寻求主的庇护,
把安宁的希望寄托于天上的父!


## 二

## 贝奥武甫来到鹿厅

就这样,哈夫丹之子赫罗斯加

190　整日忧心忡忡,那班智慧的王公
也无法为他排忧解难,因为这场灾难——
这黑暗的恐惧,降临在百姓身上,
实在太残酷,太可憎,太漫长!
格兰道尔的暴行传进高特王国,

195　传到海格拉克手下一位勇士耳里;
这位英雄出身高贵、勇猛过人,
同时代人当中堪称卓绝超凡。
他命人马上为他备好一艘快船,

good prepared;     said he battle-king

200    over swan-road     seek would,

mighty chieftain,     when he was man-needy.

That venture him     clear-sighted men

in no way blamed,     though he to them dear was;

they urged the valiant man,     omens they scanned.

205    Had the good warrior     from Geats' tribes

champions chosen     those that he bravest

find was able;     fifteen together

sea-timber sought;     warrior showed,

ocean-crafty man,     shore-boundaries.

210    Time forth passed;     ship was on waves,

boat under cliff.     Warriors willing

in prow stepped;     streams eddied,

sea against sand;     men bore

into bosom of ship     bright trappings,

215    war-gear precious;     warriors out shoved,

men on willed-way,     wood well-braced.

Went then over wave-sea     by wind urged

floater foamy-necked,     a bird most like,

until in due time     of second day

220    curved stem-post     journeyed had,

so that the sailors     land sighted,

sea-cliffs shining,     shores steep,

broad sea-nesses;     then was sea crossed,

他说他要跨过天鹅之路,

200 拜访一下那位著名的国王,

因为他此刻正需要有人出力相助。

智慧的族人中没有人说他太冒险,

虽然他们一个个与他相处亲善。

他们反而鼓励他,为他择定良辰。

205 在高特人中,贝奥武甫精心挑选

一批最勇敢的武士偕他同行,

连他自己在内,一共十五位壮士

一道奔向快船;这位老练的水手,

很快把他的勇士带到海岸。

210 良辰一到,停泊在岩石下的船只

即刻下水。武士们争先恐后

登上甲板;潮水汹涌激荡,

冲击着沙滩;勇敢的武士们

把闪光的盔甲、珍贵的兵器

215 搬进船舱;然后船儿被推进深水,

武士们开启备受祝福的航程。

木船乘着劲风,船首飞溅着浪花,

航行在大海的波涛上,它像一只鸟

在海面上飞翔,直到第二天,

220 航海者从曲颈的木舟上

已经看得见前方的陆地,

看得见闪光的岩石、高耸的山脉,

以及突兀的岬角。大海已经渡过,

voyage at ending;    thence up quickly

225    Wederas' warriors    on land stepped,

sea-timber moored;    mail shirts rattled,

battle-clothes;    God they thanked

that for them wave paths    untroubled had been.

    Then from wall saw    warden of Scyldings,

230    he who sea-cliffs    guard should,

borne over gang-plank    bright shields,

war-gear ready;    him question broke

in mind-thoughts    what these men were.

    Went him then to shore    horse riding

235    thane of Hrothgar,    strongly shook

huge spear in hands,    with speech-words asked;

    "What are you    armour-wearers,

in byrnies clad,    who thus tall keel

over sea-street    leading came,

240    hither over waters?    I long time was

coast-sitter,    sea-watch held,

so that in land of Danes    enemies any

with ship-army    ravage not might.

Not here more openly    to come began

245    shield-bearers,    nor you password

of warriors    surely not know,

nor our kinsmen's consent.    Never I bigger saw

man upon earth    than is of you one,

航程结束。高特的勇士们

225　停泊好木舟,很快登上海岸,

身上的盔甲和战袍叮当作响。

他们衷心地向上帝表示谢意,

因为他们已平安到达目的地。

这时,岸上巡逻的丹麦哨兵,

230　发现了金光闪闪的盾牌

以及全副武装的一班勇士

出现在他面前;他心中十分焦急,

急切要弄清这些人的来历。

这位赫罗斯加手下的将官

235　随即挥舞手中的长矛

驱马上前,用严厉的声音吆喝:

"你们是什么人,竟如此大胆,

全副武装乘坐高大的战船

跨洋过海侵犯我们的边界!

240　听着! 长期以来,我一直

守卫在这海岸上,负责监视

任何敌人从海上乘船而来,

把我们丹麦的领土侵犯!

从来没有持盾者像你们这样

245　明目张胆,闯入我们的地盘。

你们显然答不出军士的口令,

显然没有得到我的同胞的批准。

不过,你们那位披甲的勇士

warrior in armour;       not is this a mere retainer,

250       by weapons made worthy,       unless him his looks belie,

supreme features.       Now I your must

origin know       before you on from here

false spies       in land of Danes

further fare.       Now you far-dwellers,

255       sea-voyagers,       my hear

one-fold thought:       speed is best

to convey       whence your comings are."


Him the eldest       answered,

crew's captain       word-hoard unlocked:

260       "We are of tribe       of Geats people

and Hygelac's       hearth-companions.

Was my father       to folk well-known,

a noble fighter,       Ecgtheow named;

knew winters many       before he away passed

265       old from dwellings;       him readily recalls

wise man every       widely through world.

We with staunch intent       lord your,

son of Halfdane,       to seek have come,

people-protector;       be you to us guide good!

270       Have we to the grand       great errand

Danes' lord;       not shall there secret any

be, as I think.       You know, if it is

那么英武,这我倒从未见过,

250 如果堂皇的仪表没有骗人,我敢说,
他绝不是凭武器乔装的侍臣。
在你们从我这里继续前进以前,
我必须先弄清你们的身份,
我不能让间谍混入丹麦国土,

255 远道而来的陌生人和航海者,
请听清楚我的问题并马上回答:
你们这班人究竟来自哪里?"


航海者的首领、武士的统帅
打开言辞的宝库,这样回答:

260 "我们是高特部落的人,
我们是海格拉克国王的亲兵。
我的父亲出身高贵、大名鼎鼎,
艾克赛奥就是他的大名;
他在世生活了无数个冬天,

265 才抛下家园去世,普天下
所有的智者都对他深切怀念。
我们此行怀着友好的意愿
拜访你们的主人哈夫丹之子——
百姓的庇护人。请你指示我们:

270 我们负有伟大的使命,要见见
丹麦的国王;我觉得此事
用不着保密。你一定知道

as we truly    tell have heard,

that among Scyldings    of foes I know-not what

275    skulking scourge    in dark nights

unrolls through horror    unheard-of ruin,

scathe and slaughter.    I for-that Hrothgar may

from open heart    advice provide.

how he, wise and good,    foe can defeat-

280    if to him change    ever should.

for evils' agony    amends, in turn come-

and the care-surges    cooler grow;

or ever after    hardship-time,

sore-need suffers,    while still there stands

285    in high place    house most splendid."

    Warden spoke,    there on horse sat,

officer unafraid:    "Every shall

sharp shield-fighter    difference know

of words and deeds,    he who well thinks.

290    I it hear    that this is loyal troop

to lord of Scyldings.    Pass forth bearing

weapons and war-gear;    I you will guide;

also I kin-thanes    my will order

against foes any    vessel your

295    newly-tarred,    prow upon sand

in honour to guard,    until back it bears

over sea-streams    dear man,

我们听到的传闻是否真实：
在丹麦人中间出现了某个敌人，

275　他利用黑夜犯下可恨的罪行，
令人恐惧地宣泄他的仇恨，
施行伤害与屠杀。此行我诚心诚意
来向赫罗斯加进献良策，
帮助这位贤明的国王降伏仇敌，

280　也许他能从此时来运转，
摆脱恶魔的骚扰，并平息
他胸中无法平静的忧虑。
否则他就继续蒙受祸患，
受恶魔的压迫，只要那宏伟的大殿

285　继续高耸在丹麦的高地上。"
勇敢的哨兵坐在马背上
如此回话："每个聪慧的军士
只要他保持清醒的头脑，
便能辨别是非，判断好恶。

290　这会我明白了，你们是一支
对丹麦国王友好的队伍。
带上你们的武器，继续上路吧，
我将为你们带路，我还要吩咐
我的同胞把你们的船只——

295　那艘曲颈的木舟推上沙滩，
严加看管，以防它落入敌手，
直到它载着可敬的勇士

wood swoop-necked     to Wedermark;

of brave-doers     to such it will be granted

300     that the battle-rush     safely he survives."

They went then faring,     boat at rest waited,

rode upon rope     broad-bosomed ship

on anchor fast.     Boar-shapes shone

over cheekguards     adorned with gold,

305     bright and fire-hardened,     life-watch it held.

War-hearts aroused,     warriors hurried,

marched together     until they hall timbered

glorious and gold-decked     to glimpse were able;

that was noblest     for earth-dwellers

310     of halls under heavens,     in it the ruler lived;

blazed the light     over lands many.

To them then warlike guide     court of brave men

shining showed     that they it to might

straightway walk;     warrior worthy

315     horse turned,     words after spoke:

"Time is for me to go;     Father all-ruling

with mercy     you may keep

on journeys safe!     I to coast will go,

for hostile bands     the watch to hold."


320     Street was stone-bright,     path guided

men together.     War-byrnie shone

穿过大海返回高特国土。
但愿命运保佑如此勇敢的人
300 安然无恙度过争战的风暴。"
他们继续进发。船舱宽敞的木舟
用缆绳系住,稳稳地停泊
在沙滩上。饰有野猪图案的头盔
镶嵌着黄金,显得金光闪闪,
305 那好战的野猪似乎在为他们设防。
武士们一个个斗志昂扬,
雄赳赳地向前走,直到那座
金碧辉煌的王宫遥遥在望。
那是天地间最雄伟的建筑,
310 里面住着雄踞一方的国王,
它的光辉已把方圆数里的地面照亮。
勇敢的向导指着闪光的宫廷,
告诉他们沿着大道笔直向前,
高贵的武士然后掉转马头,
315 对他们说了这样·番话:
"我该回去了;愿全能的上帝
保佑你们诸事如意、一路平安!
我必须马上返回海岸边,
去监视可能来侵犯的敌人。"

320 脚下的大道由石块铺砌而成,
武士们沿着它列队而行。

hard hand-linked,    ring-iron shimmering

sang in armour    as they to hall first

in their grim gear    marching came.

325    They set down,sea-weary,    broad shields,

rims right-hard    against the building's wall;

bent then to bench,    byrnies rang,

war-clothes of warriors;    spears stood,

seamen's weapons    stacked together,

330    ash-wood tipped with grey;    was the iron troop

by weapons made worthy.    Then there proud hero

warrior-men    for lineage asked:

"Whence ferry you    plated shields,

grey sarks    and grim helms,

335    war-shafts' hoard?    I am Hrothgar's

spokesman and henchman.    Not saw I foreign

thus many men    bolder-looking.

Think I that you from valour,    not from exile

but from heart-urge    Hrothgar sought."

340    Him then courageous    answered

proud Wederas' prince,    words after spoke

hard under helm:    "We are Hygelac's

board-companions;    Beowulf is my name.

Wish I to say    to son of Halfdane,

345    to famed chieftain    my errand,

to leader your,    if he to us grant will

当他们雄赳赳步入大厅，

巧手织成的铠甲闪闪发光，

耀眼的铁环在战袍上歌唱。

325 久航令人生厌，他们把盾牌——

那坚固的护身物搁在墙边。

然后他们在凳子上坐下，

身上的盔甲和战袍叮当作响：

航海者的长矛排成一排，

330 那枪尖都是一色的青灰，

这样的武器值得勇士们使用。

一位高傲的丹麦人开始盘问：

"这些镶金的盾牌、灰色的盔甲，

护面的头盔和一大批长矛，

335 你们都是从什么地方带来的？

我是赫罗斯加的传令官和亲信，

我从未见过这么多勇敢的陌生人。

你们来此求见赫罗斯加，

想必为了远大志向，不是为了避难？"

340 那位以勇力著称的人回答他，

那位戴着头盔、豪迈的高特人做了回话：

"我们是海格拉克的好伙伴，

贝奥武甫就是我的名字。

如果你们伟大的国王不见外，

345 如果他答应惠然接见我们，

我将当面向哈夫丹之子

that we him, so good,     greet might."

     Wulfgar spoke,     he was Wendels' chief,

was his courage     to many known,

350     war-skill and wisdom:     "I this from friend of Danes,

lord of Scyldings,     inquire will,

from rings' bestower,     as you asking are,

from chieftain famed,     about your venture,

and you the answer     quickly tell

355     which me the good king     to give thinks fit."

     Turned then quickly     to where Hrothgar sat

old and hoary     with his heroes' band;

walked stoutly,     so that he by shoulders stood

of Danes' lord;     knew he retinue's custom.

360     Wulfgar spoke     to his friend-lord:

     "Here are journeyed,     from afar come

over ocean's sweep     Geats' men;

the eldest one     war-fighters

Beowulf name.     They asking are

365     that they, chief my,     with you might

words exchange;     not you them refusal give

of your answers,     gracious Hrothgar!

They by war-gear     worthy seem

of men's respect;     indeed the chief is manly

370     who the battle-soldiers     hither led."

向著名的首领陈述我的使命。"

温德尔人的酋长乌夫加，

人人都知道他作战勇敢、足智多谋，

350 他这样回答："应你们的请求，

我这就去请示丹麦人的朋友和国王——

那项圈的赐予者和著名的首领，

把你们的历险告诉他，并且

将国王觉得最合适的答复

355 尽快地向你们如实转达。"

他说完即刻去见赫罗斯加，

白发苍苍的老王就坐在贵胄中间；

勇武的传令官直接来到他跟前，

侍臣的礼仪他驾轻就熟。

360 乌夫加这样对他的国王说：

"一队高特人越过大海的波涛，

千里迢迢来到我们这里；

武士们用'贝奥武甫'这个名字

称呼他们的首领；我的土公，

365 他们要求您本人接见他们。

尊贵的赫罗斯加国王，

请您千万不要轻易拒绝!

这班人全身披挂，看样子

都是高贵的人，尤其那位

370 武士的首领，更是气宇非凡! "

Hrothgar spoke,     helm of Scyldings:

"I him knew     youth-being:

was his old-father     Ecgtheow called,

to whom in home gave     Hrethel of Geats

375     his only daughter;     is his heir now

hardy here come,     sought loyal friend.

Then said it     seafarers,

they who gift-coins     for Geats ferried

thither in thanks,     that he thirty

380     men's main-strength     in his hand-grip

battle-famed has.     Him holy God

in kindness     us has sent,

to West-Danes,     as I hope have,

against Grendel's terror.     I the good man shall

385     for his daring     treasures offer.

Be you in haste,     order in to go

to see kin-company     grouped together;

tell them too in words     that they are welcome

to Danes' nation."     Then to door of hall

390     Wulfgar went,     word from within announced:

"To you commands to say     victory-lord my,

leader of East-Danes,     that he your lineage knows,

and you to him are     over sea-swells

hard-minded     hither welcome.

395     Now you may go     in your war-gear,

丹麦人的保卫者赫罗斯加说:

"这个人童年时我就认识;

他的父亲名叫艾克塞奥,

高特王雷塞尔把自己的女儿

375　嫁给了他;如今他勇敢的儿子

为了友谊来到我们的国家。

我曾经派人给高特人送过礼品,

回来的人都说他战场上

英名远扬,他一只手的力量

380　就与三十个勇士的力量相当。

如今神圣而仁慈的上帝

把他派到我们丹麦人的中间,

我希望他能为我们消除

格兰道尔带来的凶险。到那时,

385　我要重重酬谢这位好人。

你们快去,把客人迎接进来,

让他们见见我手下的一班侍臣;

传我的话:丹麦全国上下

欢迎他们的光临!"乌夫加奉命

390　来到大厅门口传达国王的旨意:

"东丹麦国的首领,我的胜利之主

吩咐我向诸位传话:他认识你们的祖先,

你们此番不畏艰难渡海前来,

他谨向大家表示热烈的欢迎。

395　现在你们不必脱下身上的盔甲

under armour-masks    Hrothgar to see;

let battle-shields    here abide,

wood, slaughter-shafts,    words' outcome."

    Arose then the mighty man,    about him warriors many,

400    sturdy thanes' band;    some there waited,

war-gear guarded,    as them the hardy leader bade.

They hurried together,    them man guided

under Heorot's roof;    warrior walked

hard under helmet    so that he in hall stood.

405    Beowulf spoke,    on him byrnie shone,

armour-net woven    by smith's artifice:

    "Hail to you,Hrothgar!    I am Hygelac's

kinsman and thane;    have I great deeds many

tackled in youth.    To me became Grendel's tricks

410    on my native turf    clearly known;

say seafarers    that this hall stands,

building finest,    for warriors all,

idle and useless    when evening-light

under heaven's brightness    hidden goes.

415    Then me that advised    people my,

the best ones,    wise-minded men,

chieftain Hrothgar,    that I you sought,

because they strength's force    mine knew;

themselves had seen    when I from battles came,

420    blood-stained from enemies,    where I five bound,

就可以直接面见赫罗斯加。

但盾牌与长矛暂且留在这里,

等会见结束再任君处理。"

那勇士于是站起身,那班强健的伙伴

400　围在他的身边;一部分人留了下来,

奉勇敢的首领之命看守武器。

在传令官的指引下,他们迈开大步,

进入鹿厅;那位戴着头盔的英雄

一直来到大厅中央才停住脚步。

405　贝奥武甫开口说话,身上的盔甲闪闪发光,

那精致的环锁见证铁匠的手艺高强。

"向您致敬,赫罗斯加国王!

我是海格拉克的外甥和侍臣。

少年时代,我便建立过许多功勋。

410　格兰道尔的恶行我早有耳闻;

航海归来的人都对我说,

这座人间最漂亮的大厅,每当

夜幕降临,天光淹没在苍穹,

里面就空空荡荡,一片凄凉。

415　因此,我的同胞——那些智慧的大臣,

建议我踏上此次征程,

来此拜见您,赫罗斯加国王,

因为他们知道我力量非凡。

他们曾目睹我从战场凯旋,

420　浑身沾满血污,在一次争战中,

destroyed giants' kin,     and in waves slew

monsters by night,     gnawing torment suffered,

avenged Wederas' wrongs     —trouble they asked for—

ground down grim foes;     and now with Grendel shall,

425     with the monster     alone conclude

dispute with demon.     I you now then,

lord of Bright-Danes,     ask will,

defender of Scyldings,     one request,

that you me not refuse,     warriors' shield,

430     dear-friend of peoples,     now I thus far have come,

that I may alone     and my nobles' band,

this hardy crew,     Heorot cleanse.

     Have I also heard     that the monster

in his ragtag     weapons not heeds;

435     I it then scorn,     —so for me Hygelac may be,

my liege-lord,     in heart happy—

that I sword bear     or broad shield,

yellow-rim to battle,     but I with grip shall

fight with fiend     and for life struggle,

440     foe against foe;     there put faith must

in Lord's justice     the one that death takes.

     Think I that he will,     if he manage might,

in the war-hall     Geats' people

devour unfearing,     as he often did,

445     the muscle of noble men.     Not you my will-need

俘获了五个巨人，捣毁了巨人家族；

有天晚上，我还在波涛中历经艰难，

杀死众多海怪，替高特人报了仇——

把怪物撕成碎片——而这一次，

425　我要单独跟魔怪格兰道尔

较量一番。因此，我请求您——

丹麦人的国王，希尔德子孙的庇护人，

武士的避难所和百姓的朋友，

此次我漂洋过海远道而来，

430　请你千万不要拒绝，允许我

单独率领我手下的一班勇士

将作祟鹿厅的恶魔铲除。

我也曾听说，这个怪物一旦发怒，

任何武器都对他无济于事。

435　因此，为了让我的主公——

海格拉克为我感到欣慰，

我不屑于使用刀枪和盾牌：

我要跟恶魔来一番徒手交战，

与他针锋相对，拼个你死我活。

440　最后到底是谁被死神擒获，

那只有让上帝来为我们裁决。

我并不怀疑，如果他获得胜利，

他会在血战的大厅吞噬

高特的子民，就像他以往

445　吞噬高贵的丹麦人那样。

head to shroud,     but he me have will

in gore drenched,     if me death takes;

bears bloody corpse,     to bite intends,

eats lone-prowler     unlamenting,

450     mires his moor-lair;     not you for my will-need

body's welfare     longer grieve.

Send to Hygelac,     if me war takes,

battle-shroud best,     that my breast protects,

of garments finest;     it is Hrethel's legacy,

455     Weland's handiwork.     Goes always fate as she must!"


Hrothgar spoke,     helm of Scyldings:

     "For war-fights you,     friend my Beowulf,

and for favour     us have sought.

Kindled your father     feud greatest;

460     was he Heatholaf's     hand-slayer

among the Wylfings;     then him Wederas' kin

for war-fear     shelter were unable.

Thence he sought     South-Danes' folk

over waves' surging,     Honour-Scyldings;

465     then I first ruled     folk of Danes

and in youth held     precious kingdom,

hoard-fort of heroes;     then was Heorogar dead,

my elder brother     unliving,

son of Halfdane;     he was better than I.

如果我死了,你们无须把尸体掩埋,

那时我一定被咬得血肉模糊。

他会把我的尸体带走,返回

他居住的巢穴,然后残忍地

450　大吃大嚼。你们再用不着

为我的尸体费心。如果我打败了,

就请派人把我这一身漂亮的盔甲

交还给海格拉克国王,因为

它是雷塞尔的馈赠,威兰德①的杰作

455　命中注定的事,你无法抗拒。"

① 古代斯堪的纳维亚人的冶炼神。

丹麦人的庇护者赫罗斯加说:

"我的朋友贝奥武甫,你来我们这里

为的是建立功勋和过去的友谊。

你父亲曾经惹过一桩大血仇,

460　他亲手杀死威尔芬人希塞拉夫。

高特王国当时因为害怕战争,

没敢把他留在国内。因此,

他只好越过汹涌的波涛

来投奔光荣的希尔德子孙。

465　那时我年纪尚轻,刚刚登基

接手治理丹麦——这珍贵的王国,

英雄聚集的城堡。哈夫丹之子——

我的兄长希罗加刚刚去世,

他是一位比我更优秀的国王。

470      Then the feud      with fees I settled;

sent I to Wylfings      over water's ridge

old treasures;      Ecgtheow me oaths swore.

Sorrow is me to say      in heart my

to man any      what me Grendel has

475      hurts in Heorot      with his hate-thoughts

swift onslaughts caused;      is my hall-troop,

war-band, waned;      them fate swept away

in Grendel's grisliness.      God easily can

the mad slayer's      deeds curtail.

480      Full often vowed      on beer drunk,

over ale-cup      battle-fighters,

that they in beer-hall      abide would

Grendel's onslaught      with grim swords.

Then was this mead-hall      in morning time

485      great-house gore-stained      when day lightened,

all bench-wood      with blood beslimed,

hall battle-gory;      had I friends the fewer,

precious retinue,      for these death took away.

Sit now to feast      and untie thoughts,

490      victory-fame,to men,      as your heart urges."

470    后来我用金钱化解了那桩血仇。
       我派人渡海把财宝送给威尔芬人,
       你父亲从此与我起誓结盟。
       说起格兰道尔,我的心里
       好不悲伤! 他怀着仇恨之心

475    在鹿厅滥施暴行,给我带来
       莫大的耻辱。大厅的卫兵、战士
       一天天减少。命运把他们一个个
       卷进格兰道尔的魔掌。当然,
       上帝定能阻止屠杀者的疯狂。

480    我的将士们一旦喝得酩酊大醉,
       常常赌咒发誓:他们要持刀剑
       守候在大厅,等待格兰道尔,
       与他比个高低。然而,第二天一早,
       但见宴乐厅里又是血迹斑斑,

485    长凳上沾满血污,湿漉漉一片,
       整个大厅随处都是凝固的血块。
       我的朋友和忠诚的侍从日益减少,
       因为死神已把他们一一带走。
       现在请诸位入席,如果有兴致,

490    再谈谈你们的想法和英雄的业绩。"

# PART THREE
## The Feast at Heorot

Then was for Geat-men      together grouped

in beer-hall      on bench made-room;

there the strong-hearted      to sit down went,

in prowess proud.      Thane duty held,

495      he who in hands bore      ornate ale-cup,

poured bright drink.      Poet at times sang

clear in Heorot.      There was heroes' joy,

host not small      of Danes and Wederas.


Unferth spoke,      Ecglaf's son,

500      who at feet sat      of lord of Scyldings,

he unbound battle-words;      was for him Beowulf's venture,

brave seafarer's,      great bitterness,

because he not allowed      that any other man

ever great deeds the more      on middle-earth

505      achieved under heavens      than he himself:

"Are you the Beowulf      who with Breca fought,

on broad sea      at swimming raced,

where you arrogantly      oceans tested

and for silly boast      in deep water

# 三
## 鹿厅盛宴

他们于是在宴乐厅为高特人
腾出座位。勇士们一个个
气宇轩昂，坐到各自的座位上。
这时有一位执勤的侍臣
495　　端上一只镂金的大酒杯，
给他们倒上美酒。吟游诗人
则放声歌唱。丹麦人与高特人
一起饮宴作乐，那气氛好不欢畅！

坐在丹麦国王身边的安佛斯——
500　　艾格拉夫之子这时挑衅；
贝奥武甫这位勇敢水手的壮举
深深刺痛了他的心，因为
他不愿看见别人比他更荣耀，
普天下不管谁取得成就，
505　　都会使他感到十分难受：
"你就是那位跟布雷克争胜，
在茫茫大海上游泳的贝奥武甫？
是你为了虚荣潜入大海探险，
为了愚蠢的吹牛把自己的性命

| 510 | with lives juggled? | Not you any man, |
| | not friend nor foe, | dissuade was able |
| | from sorry exploit | when you in sea swam; |
| | there you tide-streams | in arms embraced, |
| | measured sea-roads, | with arms thrashed, |
| 515 | glided over ocean; | water in surges welled, |
| | in winter's swells. | You in water's grasp |
| | seven nights strove; | he you in swimming overcame, |
| | had more strength. | Then him in morning-time |
| | on Heatho-Reams' coast | the sea up cast; |
| 520 | thence he sought | sweet homeland, |
| | dear to his people, | land of Brondings, |
| | stronghold fine, | where he folk had, |
| | fortress and rings. | Boast all with you |
| | the son of Beanstan | truly kept. |
| 525 | Then expect I for you | worse result, |
| | although you battle-clashes | everywhere survived, |
| | grim warfare, | if you for Grendel dare |
| | night-long time | nearby to wait." |
| | Beowulf spoke, | son of Ecgtheow: |
| 530 | "What! you very much, | friend my Unferth, |
| | on beer drunk, | of Breca have talked, |
| | told about his venture. | Truth I claim, |
| | that I sea-strength | greater had, |
| | hardships in waves, | than any other man. |

510 当成儿戏？当你决意下海，
　　不管是谁，无论是仇是友，
　　都无法劝说你把计划放弃。
　　你用双臂拥抱大海的浪花，
　　用胳膊丈量海水，挥舞双手

515 滑行在海洋上；冰冷的海水
　　波涛汹涌。你在大海的巨掌里
　　挣扎了七天。但结果大海胜了你，
　　因为它更强大。第二天一早，
　　大海把他抛上希塞里姆海岸。

520 他从那里开始返乡的路程，
　　回到布朗丁人可爱的家园，
　　坚固的堡垒，那里有他的乡亲、
　　城堡和财宝。那位比斯丹之子
　　对你夸下的海口得到了证实。

525 因此，如果你胆敢在格兰道尔身边
　　待上一个晚上，我可以预见：
　　你的结局一定很不幸——尽管你
　　在别的争战中一次次保住了性命。"
　　艾克塞奥之子贝奥武甫说：

530 "哟，我的朋友安佛斯，你唠唠叨叨
　　说了那么多有关布雷克的话，
　　你一定喝醉了，我可以告诉你真相：
　　比起你所提到的那个人，
　　在海上我确实更强大，历险更多。

535    We it agreed,      lads-being,

and vaunted     —were both then still

in youth-life—     that we on ocean out

lives should risk,    and that we did thus.

We had swords naked    when we in sea swam,

540    hard in hands;    we us against whales

to defend thought.    Not he at all from me

on flood-waves far    to float was able,

swifter on sea,    nor I from him would part.

Then we together    on sea were

545    five nights' span,    until us current parted,

waves wallowing,    of weathers coldest,

darkening night,    and north wind

battle-keen against us turned:    cruel were waves.

Was sea-fishes'    anger stirred;

550    there me against foes    body-sark my

hard hand-linked    help provided,

battle-dress braided    on breast lay,

gold-adorned.    Me to depth dragged

fierce foe-scather,    firmly had me

555    grim in grasp;    yet to me granted was

that I monster    with spear-point pierced,

with battle-blade;    fray-clash destroyed

mighty mere-beast    through my hand.

535　我们像孩子一样吹嘘打赌——
　　　当年我们两人的确年纪尚轻——
　　　决计拿生命在大海上冒险，
　　　这事我们而且说到做到。
　　　游泳时我们手上握着宝剑，

540　以便在鲸鱼向我们袭击时，
　　　用来保护自己。在大海的波涛上，
　　　他根本无法超到我的前面，
　　　而我也未能把他抛在背后。
　　　整整五天五夜，我们并肩前进，

545　直到汹涌的潮水把我们分开。
　　　当时海浪滔天，天气寒冷，
　　　北风呼啸，黑夜渐次深沉，
　　　一切都于我们不利，大海凶险无比。
　　　海怪此时也被惹得怒气冲冲；

550　多亏有坚固的盔甲保护着
　　　我的身体，使我免遭他们的袭击，
　　　镶金的护胸甲为我抵御
　　　来犯之敌。然而，一头凶残的怪兽
　　　还是把我紧紧抓住，并把我

555　拖进大海的深渊；幸好，
　　　我及时腾出手，用锋利的宝剑
　　　向那头怪物刺去；就这样，
　　　我亲手铲除了一头海中巨兽。

Thus me often      loathed-attackers

560    threatened savagely.    I them served

with precious sword,    as it fitting was.

Not they of the feast    rejoicing had,

crime-creatures,    that they me devoured,

banquet sat round    on sea-bed near;

565    but in morning    by blades wounded

on ebb shore    up they lay,

by swords put to sleep,    so that since never

on steep water    sea-travellers'

course they balked.    Light from east came,

570    bright beacon of God,    waves subsided,

so that I sea-nesses    to sight was able,

windswept rock-walls.    Fate often spares

undoomed hero    when his heart endures.

Yet my luck was    that I with sword slew

575    monsters nine.    Not I by night heard

under heaven's hollow    harder fight,

nor on tide-streams    more hard-pressed man;

yet I foes' grasp    alive escaped,

from exploit weary.    Then me sea swept off,

580    flood along current    to Lapps' land,

waves wallowing.    Nothing I about you

of such deadly combats    tell have heard,

blades' terror.    Breca never yet

别的海怪来势汹汹,继续向我

560 频频攻击。但我不失时机
挥舞宝剑跟他们周旋。
这班食人怪兽未能如愿以偿
在海底围着我举行盛宴,
把我当成他们的美餐。相反,

565 第二天早上,他们带着致命伤
被海水冲上岸,就此长眠不醒,
从那以后,在大海的深渊,
他们再不能兴风作浪,阻挡
航海者的行程。上帝的明灯

570 从东方升起,大海复归宁静,
我又能看见前方的陆地,以及
迎风的峭壁。只要他意志坚强,
命运之神常常放过不甘失败的英雄。
不管怎么说,我用我的宝剑

575 杀死了九个海怪。我从未听说
天底下有谁经历过更艰苦的夜战,
有谁在海里遭际更多的凶顽。
筋疲力竭的我活着逃出
敌人的魔掌。然后汹涌的海浪

580 托起我的身子,把我带到
芬兰人的土地。而我从未听说
你也经历过如此激烈的争战,
如此可怕的冒险。布雷克也从未

in battle-play,     nor either of you,

585    so bold a    deed performed

with shining swords     —not I of it much boast—

but you your brothers'    killer were,

close kinsmen;    for that you in hell shall

torment suffer,    though your mind is strong.

590      Tell I you in truth,    son of Ecglaf,

that never Grendel so many    grim deeds had done,

terrible monster,    to leader your,

hurt in Heorot,    if your courage were,

heart so battle-fierce    as you yourself say;

595    but he has found    that he the fight not needs,

terrible sword-storm    of your nation

greatly to dread,    of Victory-Scyldings;

he takes forced toll,    to none shows mercy

in nation of Danes,    but he pleasure takes,

600    slays and slices,    fight not expects

from Spear-Danes.    But I him Geats' shall

strength and courage    before long now,

in battle offer.    Will go back he who may

to mead exulting,    when morning-light

605    over men's sons    of another day,

sun bright-clothed    from south shines."

    Then was happy    treasure's giver

old-haired and war-brave;    for aid trusted

参加过这样的战斗,无论你还是他

585　都没有用宝剑建立过辉煌的功绩——

我并没有过分夸耀我自己。

而你只会屠杀你的同胞兄弟,

由于那桩罪行,你将永远

受地狱之苦,你的聪明也救不了你。

590　我跟你说句实话,艾格拉夫之子,

如果你在战场上十分勇敢,正如

你自己声称的那样,魔怪格兰道尔

对你的主公就无法犯下这么多罪行,

就不能把鹿厅搅得鲜血淋淋。

595　正因他发现他用不着害怕

与你们的人交战,用不着提防

胜利的希尔德子孙的刀剑,

他才强行征税,对你们丹麦人

毫不留情;他从此随心所欲,

600　大肆杀戮,从不指望你们

会奋起抵抗。如今我要让他看看

高特人在战场上的勇气和力量。

当明晨的天光,那火红的太阳

从南方照临人类的子孙,那时,

605　人们只要乐意,就可喜气洋洋,

回到宴乐大厅作乐寻欢。"

财宝的赐主,白发苍苍的老英雄

听后十分高兴;丹麦人的国王

chief of Bright-Danes;     heard in Beowulf

610    folk's keeper    firm-resolved intent.

      There was heroes' laughter,   noise resounded,

words were joyful.    Walked Wealhtheow forth,

queen of Hrothgar,    of kindness mindful,

greeted, gold-adorned,    warriors in hall,

615    and then noble lady   goblet handed

first to East-Danes'   land-protector,

bade him be happy   at the beer-taking,

by nation loved;   he in delight took

feast and hall-cup,   victorious king.

620    Went among then   lady of Helmings

veterans and youth   alike to each,

gold-cups handed,   until time came

that she to Beowulf,   ring-adorned queen

in spirit thriving,   mead-cup carried;

625    she greeted Geats' chief,   God thanked,

wise in words,   for that which with her wish agreed,

that she in any   man believed

from onslaughts for relief.   He the cup took,

slaughter-fierce warrior,   from Wealhtheow,

630    and then gave voice,   for war made eager.

      Beowulf spoke,   son of Ecgtheow:

      "I it planned   when I on ocean put out,

in sea-boat settled   with my wamor band,

有了指望;百姓的庇护人

610　听见了贝奥武甫坚定的声音。
　　英雄们一个个喜笑颜开,大伙
　　吵吵嚷嚷,好不欢畅! 这时,
　　打扮得珠光宝气的王后维瑟欧
　　彬彬有礼地上前与众人见面。

615　高贵的夫人首先把酒敬给
　　东丹麦王国的卫士,祝愿他
　　欢欢喜喜享用美酒,永远受
　　人民的爱戴。胜利的国王
　　高高兴兴接过酒杯一饮而尽。

620　丹麦人的主妇,佩金戴银的王后
　　然后端着金制的酒杯走上前来,
　　向在座的新老侍臣一一敬酒,
　　直到她满面春风,款款来到
　　贝奥武甫跟前。她以优雅的言辞,

625　向这位高特人的首领致意,
　　感谢上帝使她了却心愿,
　　使她能够信赖可靠的英雄,
　　帮他们铲除祸患。骁勇的武士
　　从维瑟欧手中接过酒杯,

630　他已做好准备,随时可以参战。
　　艾克塞奥之子贝奥武甫这样说:
　　"我在踏上航程,与我的伙伴
　　坐进船舱的那一刻,就已下定决心,

that I properly       your people's

635  wishes should perform,       or in slaughter fall

in foe's grip fixed.       I achieve shall

daring deed,       or else death-day

in this mead-hall       my endure."

　　　The woman the words       well liked,

640  boast-speech of the Geat;       went gold-adorned

noble folk-queen       by her lord to sit.

　　　Then were again as before       inside hall

bold words spoken,       people happy,

victory-folk's clamour,       until before long

645  son of Halfdane       seek wished

evening rest;       knew the monster

for the high hall       combat planned,

since when they sun's light       to see were able

until darkening       night over all,

650  shadow-helm's shapes       sliding came

dark under clouds.       Band all rose up.

Greeted then       man the other,

Hrothgar Beowulf,       and him luck wished,

wine-hall's rule,       and these words spoke:

655  　　　"Never I to any man       before entrusted,

since I hand and shield       to raise was able,

strong-hall of Danes       save to you now.

Have now and hold       house most noble,

我要解救你们的人民，否则

635　　就让我在血腥的屠杀中倒下，

在仇敌的魔爪中死于非命。

我要么创建一件英雄的业绩，

要么让这座宴乐厅见证我的末日。"

王后听了高特人的豪言壮语，

640　　感到十分满意；这位高贵的妇人

然后就坐回到国王的身边。

大厅里再次响起热烈的交谈声，

大家七嘴八舌，沸反盈天，

直到哈夫丹之子赫罗斯加

645　　发布安寝的旨意；他知道，

魔怪对鹿厅早已虎视眈眈，

白昼的光芒一旦变成黑暗，

将所有的物体吞没，黑夜中

憧憧鬼影——乌云下那黑色的幽灵

650　　将蠢蠢欲动，出来作祟行凶。

所有的人都从座位上站起，

赫罗斯加再次向贝奥武甫

表示敬意，祝他福星高照，

看管好宴乐厅。赫罗斯加说：

655　　"如果我自己仍挥得动刀枪，

我决不会把这雄伟的大厅

托付别人，现在我把它托付给你。

请你把这座大厦好好看管，

keep mind on valour,      strong courage show,

660    watch against foe.     Not will you desires lack

if you the courage-deed      alive endure."

# PART FOUR
## The Fight with Grendel

Then Hrothgar went      with his heroes' band,

defender of Scyldings      out from hall;

wished war-chief      Wealhtheow to seek,

665    queen as bed-mate.      Had King of glory

Grendel against,      as men have heard,

hall-guard set;      special task held

for chief of Danes,      monster-guard he kept.

Indeed Geats' leader      gladly trusted

670    mighty strength,      Ruler's favour.

Then he from him took      iron-byrnie,

helm from head,      handed his gorgeous sword,

of irons choicest,      to servant-thane,

and him to guard commanded      battle-gear.

记住你的英名,表现你的勇气,
660 严防仇敌侵犯。我会重重赏你,
只要你今晚能安然无恙。"

# 四
## 贝奥武甫战格兰道尔

丹麦人的保护者赫罗斯加
率领他的侍臣离开大厅。
国王去会晤他的王后维瑟欧,
665 与她同床就寝。正如上文所言,
光荣的国王已经派出卫士
去对付格兰道尔;他交给贝奥武甫
一项特殊使命:对魔怪严加防范。
高特人的首领心中好不欢喜,
670 因为丹麦王坚信他的勇力。
他于是脱下战袍,摘下头盔,
连同那把用纯钢制作的宝剑,
交给一位卫兵,并嘱咐他
把这些武器仔细看护。

675     Spoke then the good man     boast-words some,

Beowulf of Geets,     before he in bed stepped:

     "Not I me in war-strength     wenker reckon

in battle-deeds     than Grendel him;

and so l him with sword     weary not-will,

680     of life deprive,     though I surely might;

not knows he the good skills     so that he me back may strike,

shield hack,     although he famous is

for deadly tricks;     but we at night shall

sword forsake     if he seek dares

685     war without weapons,     and then wise God

on whichever hand     holy Lord

honour will allot     as him fitting seems."

     Bent then war-bold man,     bolster received

warrior's cheek,     and him around many a

690     sturdy seaman     in hall-sleep settled.

Not any of them thought     that he thence should

again loved country     ever visit,

folk or noble fort,     where he nurtured was;

for they had heard     that them already far too many

695     in that wine-hall     bloody death destroyed,

Danes' people.     But them Lord granted

war-luck's webs,     to Wederas' men,

solace and support,     so that they foe their

through one's strength     all overcame,

675　　高特的贝奥武甫上床以前，
　　　　再次说出这样的壮语豪言：
　　　　"我敢说，论勇气，论本领，
　　　　我都不在格兰道尔之下；因此，
　　　　我将不用剑取他的性命，

680　　尽管那样做对我确实危险。
　　　　虽然他穷凶极恶，但他不懂得
　　　　如何使用武器跟我作战，不知道
　　　　如何把我的盾牌劈成碎片。
　　　　因此，今天晚上我们要把剑

685　　抛在一边——如果他敢徒手作战——
　　　　就让贤明的上帝，神圣的主
　　　　来主持公道，决定荣耀的归属。"
　　　　勇敢的战士于是躺下身子，
　　　　把头靠在枕头上，在他的周围

690　　他的伙伴，那班勇敢的水手也躺了下来。
　　　　大家都觉得他从此再见不到
　　　　可爱的家乡，再见不到父老乡亲，
　　　　再见不到养育他的土地，因为
　　　　他们心里清楚，在这宴乐厅，

695　　死于非命的丹麦人已不计其数。然而，
　　　　主已为他们织成幸运之网，
　　　　为高特人带来安慰和援助，
　　　　保证他们凭借一人的神威，
　　　　依靠他单独的力量克敌制胜。

700    by his own might.    Truth is revealed

that mighty God    mankind

has ruled forever.    Came in dark night

striding shadow-walker.    Sharp-shooters slept

who the horned-house    hold safe must,

705    all save one.    It was to men known

that them not could,    when Ruler not wished,

the sin-scather    under shadows drag;

but he watching    for foe in anger

waited in rising rage    for battle's outcome.


710    Then came from moor    under mist-hills

Grendel going,    God's anger he bore;

meant the killer    mankind's

specimen to snare    in hall the high.

Waded under clouds    until he wine-hall,

715    gold-house of men,    most-clearly sighted

golden gleaming.    Not was it first time

that he Hrothgar's    home had sought;

never he in life-days    before nor since

harder luck nor    hall-thanes found.

720    Came then to building    creature creeping,

from joys cut-off.    Door soon gave way,

with forged-bars fixed,    when he it with hands struck;

ripped open then death-minded,    now he enraged was,

700 这个事例足以证明一个真理：
　　我们人类的命运永远掌握在
　　全能的上帝手里。黑夜的独行者
　　这时正悄悄行走。守卫大厅的勇士
　　除了其中一位，都已呼呼入睡。

705 众所周知，只要万能的主不答应，
　　凶狠的恶魔就无法把任何人
　　拖进黑暗的深渊。贝奥武甫
　　没有睡着，他怀着满腔的愤怒，
　　等待与凶恶的敌人舍命一搏。

710 格兰道尔背负着上帝的怒火
　　走出小山脚下雾气腾腾的沼泽地。
　　可恶的掠夺者打定主意，
　　要在雄伟的大厅杀戮生灵。
　　他在云雾中潜行，直到清楚看见

715 那座金碧辉煌的宴乐厅——
　　财物的宝库。赫罗斯加的门户
　　他早已不是初次造访；然而，
　　在他的一生中，如此不走运，
　　遭遇这么多勇士，倒是第一次。

720 被剥夺了欢乐的怪物爬行着
　　来到大厅。铁环紧扣的大门
　　被他用手一碰就摇晃起来，
　　他杀气腾腾地把门拉开，

building's mouth.　　Straight after that

725　on shining floor　　foe trampled.

walked angrily;　　him from eyes stood,

flame most-like,　　light unlovely.

Saw he in chamber　　warriors many,

sleeping kin-troop　　grouped together,

730　warriors' host.　　Then his heart laughed;

meant that he should tear　　before day came,

dreadful monster,　　from every man

life from limb,　　now that him landed was

feast-meal's chance.　　Not was it his fate again

735　that he more could　　of mankind

devour after that night.　　Powerful watched to see

kinsman of Hygelac　　how the killer

with swift attacks　　engage would.

Not it the monster　　to delay intended

740　but he snatched fast　　first time

sleeping warrior,　　slashed unhindered,

bit bone-locks,　　blood from veins drank,

great chunks gorged;　　soon he had

unliving man　　entire devoured,

745　feet and hands.　　Forth nearer stepped,

took then with hand　　thought-sturdy

warrior from rest,　　reached for him

foe with open-palm;　　he spotted quickly

然后就怒气冲冲地踏上

725　　闪闪发光的地板。他的眼睛
　　　像一团燃烧的火焰，发出
　　　恶浊的光芒。他看见大厅里
　　　躺着许多人：一大班武士
　　　挤在一起，一个个睡得正香。

730　　见此情景他不由得暗自庆幸。
　　　可怕的恶魔心里盘算：天亮以前
　　　他就可以让每个人的生命
　　　与自己的肉体分离，从而获得
　　　享受盛宴的良机。只可惜

735　　他的命运不济，这一夜以后，
　　　他将再吃不到人肉。那勇士——
　　　海格拉克的亲属，正密切注视
　　　这凶手如何发动突然袭击。
　　　只见这恶魔一刻也不迟缓，

740　　迅速抓住一个沉睡的武士，
　　　急切撕裂他的肢体，咬断他的锁骨，
　　　吮吸他的鲜血，吞食他的肌肉；
　　　转眼之间，他已把整具尸体
　　　从头到脚吃得一干二净。

745　　他然后步步逼近，他的手臂
　　　触到了躺在床上的英雄，
　　　他向勇士伸出了魔爪；然而，
　　　贝奥武甫眼明手快，猛一使劲，

malice-thoughts    and on arm clasped.

750    At once it found    felonies' master,

that he had not met    on middle-earth

in world's expanse,    in other man

hand-grip harder;    he in heart grew

craven at core;    none the sooner get away he might.

755    Thought was in him hence-keen,    wished in dark to flee,

seek devils' throng;    not was his welcome there

like he in life-days    ever had met.

    Remembered then the good    kinsman of Hygelac

evenmg speech,    upright stood

760    and him firmly grasped;    fingers burst;

monster was striving outwards,    man forward stepped.

Meant the monster,    if he might so,

remoter refuge find    and away thence

flee to fen-lairs;    knew his fingers' strength

765    in enemy's grip.    That was bitter journey

that the marauder    to Heorot had made.

    Clan-hall thundered;    Danes all were,

camp-dwellers,    bold heroes all,

warriors in deadly terror.    Enraged were both

770    fierce hall-guards.    Building resounded.

    Then was wonder great    that the wine-hall

withstood battle-fighters,    that it to earth not fell,

fair building;    but it so firmly was

反将恶魔的手臂紧紧抓住。

750　恶贯满盈的魔鬼很快发现，
　　　在人世间，在这广袤的大地上，
　　　他从未遇见有谁的臂力
　　　能与此人一较高低。恶魔心里
　　　害怕起来，但已无法挣脱。

755　他真想逃回他的栖身地，回到
　　　魔鬼的群体。在他的一生中，
　　　这一次的遭遇与以往大不相同。
　　　海格拉克的外甥想起当晚的誓言，
　　　随即一跃而起，把恶魔牢牢抓住，

760　格兰道尔的手指咔嚓一声断裂。
　　　怪物向后退去，勇士紧紧跟随。
　　　恶魔千方百计想脱身，
　　　从宴乐厅返回他的沼泽地，
　　　他知道，他手指的力量已丧失在

765　敌人的手里。可恶的掠夺者
　　　此次鹿厅之行真够晦气。
　　　宴乐厅响声震天。所有的人，
　　　包括大厅卫兵，勇敢的将士，
　　　都心存恐惧。两个对手怒火冲天，

770　展开生死对抗，格斗声在大厅回响。
　　　宴乐厅竟能承受如此激烈的战斗
　　　而没有倒塌，真是奇迹一桩。
　　　亏得这大厦的里里外外

inside and out     with iron-bonding

775    skilfully constructed.     There from sill broke up

mead-bench many,     as I heard tell,

gold-decorated,     where the fighters struggled.

It not thought before     wise men of Scyldings,

that it ever by normal means     men any,

780    brilliant and bone-adorned,     batter might,

deftly destroy,     unless fire's embrace

should swallow it in flame.     Sound up arose,

new, insistent;     in North-Danes sprang

ghastly terror,     in one and all

785    of those who from wall     wailing heard,

grim-dirge groaning     God's adversary,

defeated song,     wound bemoaning

hell's captive.     Held him fast

he who of men was     in might strongest

790    on that day     of this life.


Would not earls' protector     for any cause

the lethal guest     alive release,

nor his life-days     to people any

useful he reckoned.     There many brandished,

795    warriors of Beowulf,     ancient swords,

wished prince-lord's     life protect,

famed chieftain's,     if they could so.

都有铁环加固,铁匠用精湛的技艺

775　把它建起。当他俩搏斗时——

我听说——许多镶嵌黄金的凳子

都被他们压坏,地上一片狼藉。

没有一个聪明的丹麦人曾经想过

有谁一旦脾气发作,就有力量

780　把镶骨的凳子毁坏,除非他

放一把火,让火焰在拥抱中

把它吞没。格斗声越来越响,

声音十分怪异。丹麦人大为恐慌。

围墙边传来一阵阵哀鸣,

785　听见的人个个毛骨悚然。

原来,那上帝的仇人在唱悲歌,

在唱败阵的丧曲——地狱的奴隶

因痛苦而哀哀哭叫。贝奥武甫

一直牢牢地抓住他不放,

790　他的神力真是盖世无双!


武士的庇护人无论如何不愿意

让嗜杀成性的来客活着逃离,

他觉得,恶魔的生命对任何人

都有害无益。贝奥武甫手下的武士

795　这时也都挥舞手中的宝剑

上前助阵,只要力所能及,

他们会全力以赴,希望保护

They it not knew     when they fray joined,

hard-minded     battle-fighters,

800     and on hand each     to hew resolved,

Grendel's soul to seek,     that the sin-scather

any on earth     of irons best,

of war-blades none     wound would not;

but he victory-weapons     bewitched had,

805     edges all.     Must his life-departure

on that day     of this life

wretched be,     and the alien spirit

into fiends' power     far-off travel.

Then it found,     he who many before

810     mind's miseries     on mankind,

crimes committed     —he clashed with God—

that him the body     obey would not,

but him the keen     kinsman of Hygelac

had by hand;     was each by other

815     living loathed.     Limb-pain felt

dreadful monster;     him on shoulder was

huge-wound seen,     sinews sprang apart,

burst bone-locks.     To Beowulf was

war-glory given;     must Grendel thence

820     life-sick flee     under fen-slopes,

seek joyless home;     knew more surely

that his life's was     end arrived,

他们的首领,著名的王子。

无所畏惧的武士参加战斗,

800　从四面攻击恶魔,想夺取他的性命。

但他们万万没有料到,人世间

没有一件武器,没有一把宝剑

能伤害这个作恶多端的怪物;

他有魔法护身,任何刀刃对他无碍。

805　不过,他依然保不住自己的性命,

他的死亡早已命中注定,

这来自异域的精灵势必

一步步走向遥远的地狱。

格兰道尔曾经给人类带来

810　诸多痛苦,犯下不计其数的罪行——

他存心与上帝对抗——如今

却发现自己有劲使不上,因为

海格拉克英勇卓绝的外甥

一直把他牢牢抓住。双方都想

815　置对手于死地。凶残的恶魔

已感疼痛难忍,他的肩膀

豁开一个大口,筋肉已经绽开,

锁骨已经拉断。争战的光荣

属于贝奥武甫。格兰道尔只得

820　带着致命的创伤急急逃回

阴沉沉的沼泽地。他心里清楚

他的生命已经到了尽头:

days' day-count.     For Danes all was

after the death-clash     desire fulfilled.

825     Had then purged     he who first from afar came,

shrewd and strong-hearted,     hall of Hrothgar,

rescued from ruin.     In night's-work he rejoiced,

in courage-deeds.     Had to East-Danes

Geat-men's leader     vow fulfilled,

830     so too anguish     all assuaged,

bitter sorrow,     which they before endured

and in stern duress     suffer must,

torment unlittle.     That was token clear,

when battle-brave man     hand set up,

835     arm and shoulder;     there was all together

Grendel's grip     under gaping roof.

# PART FIVE

## Celebration at Heorot

Then was in morning,     as I heard tell,

around the gift-hall     warrior many;

他大限将至。经过这场血战，
丹麦人终于实现自己的愿望。

825　来自远方那智勇双全的勇士
为赫罗斯加的大厅铲除了孽障，
使它免遭毁亡。此次夜战
使贝奥武甫感到十分自豪，
因为这位高特人的首领

830　兑现了自己的诺言，从而
将丹麦人长期忍受的痛苦与悲伤，
那无法回避的重重灾难
一概予以消除。作为见证，
勇敢的战士在宴乐大厅

835　举起格兰道尔的手臂与肩膀，
这份战利品就来自恶魔身上。

# 五

# 鹿厅祝捷

我听人们这样说，第二天早上
宴乐厅的四周围满了无数武士。

fared folk-chiefs    from far and near

840    through wide-ways    the wonder to survey,

foe's footprints.    Not his life's end

sorry seemed    to fellow any

of those who beaten foe's    track observed,

how he weary-hearted    away thence,

845    in fight defeated,    to monsters' mere

doomed and driven back,    life-trails bore.

There was in blood    water welling,

dread waves' swirl    all mingled

with scalding gore,    with sword-juice it seethed;

850    death-doomed he hid,    then, pleasure-deprived,

in fen-lair    life he laid down,

heathen soul;    there hell enfolded him.

Thence back travelled    old retainers,

so too young many    from sport-ride,

855    from lake exultant,    horses riding,

soldiers on steeds.    There was Beowulf's

triumph tongued,    many often said

that south nor north    between the seas

in whole wide earth    other not any

860    under sky's expanse    superior was

of shield-carriers,    of kingdom worthier.

Not they however friend-lord    the least blamed,

glad Hrothgar,    for he was good king.

部落的首领从四面八方赶来，

840　想看看这桩奇迹，以及恶魔
留下的足印。当人们仔细察看
失败的仇敌所走过的路线，
了解他如何带着伤口，拖着
垂死的步伐，心情懊丧地逃回

845　他那水中的老巢等待死亡，
没有人对他的厄运表示哀叹。
人们发现，那湖水波浪汹涌，
早已被鲜血染红，漩涡中
翻滚着热气腾腾的血泡。

850　他必死无疑，在沼泽地的兽穴里，
那异教的灵魂交出了自己的生命，
再得不到欢乐：他已走进地狱之门。
这一群寻踪的人——他们中
有许多年轻人——个个兴高采烈，

855　骑着骏马从湖边返回鹿厅。
一路上他们七嘴八舌，谈论着
贝奥武甫的胜利，许多人说，
无论从南到北，海内海外，
在全世界，在这广袤的天地间，

860　没有一个人能比他更强大，
比他更善战，更善于治国安邦。
不过，他们对自己的恩主赫罗斯加
并无半点诽谤，因为他是个好国王。

At times warriors     gallop let,

865     in contest race     fallow horses,

where to them earth-roads     easy seemed,

most well-known.     At times king's thane,

man word-laden,     songs recalling,

he who very many     ancient stories

870     scores remembered,     words new devised

correctly linked;     man in turn began

the feat of Beowulf     skilfully to recite,

and artfully create     a tale in keeping,

words varying;     likewise told

875     what he of Sigmund     tell had heard,

daring deeds,     wonders many,

Wæls's son's strife,     wide journeys,

those which men's sons     by no means knew,

feuds and feats of arms,     except Fitela with him,

880     when he such matters     say would,

uncle to his nephew,     since they always were

in conflict every     comrades in need;

they had great many     of giants kin

with swords subdued.     For Sigmund sprang up

885     after death-day     fame unlittle,

when war-hard warrior     serpent killed,

hoard's guardian;     he under grey stone,

prince's son     alone ventured

武士们还时而快马加鞭，

865　在平坦的道路上你追我赶，

比试谁的骑术更其高明。

人群中有一位国王的侍从

善于吟诗歌唱，他能背诵

许许多多古代的历险与武功，

870　能用精美的语句编写新词；

这时他更开始吟诵贝奥武甫的

武功事迹，用精彩的文字

巧妙地编成易记易诵的故事。

他还用相似的方式歌唱了

875　传闻中西格蒙德的英雄事迹，后代人

已经一概不知这位威尔斯之子，

不知道他的许多奇事趣闻，包括

他的游历、血仇和武功业绩；

西格蒙德曾把自己的经历

880　一五一十告诉他的外甥菲特拉，

他们甥舅两人同甘共苦，

在战场上总是相互照应。

他们用手中的剑，曾征服

许多巨人部落。西格蒙德去世后，

885　他的声名远远传播，人们称颂

这位勇敢的武士杀死毒龙——

那财宝的卫士。那次历险，

菲特拉不在他身边，勇敢的王子

fearless deed,    not was him Fitela with;

890    yet his luck was    that the sword transfixed

stupendous serpent    so that it in wall stood fast,

lordly iron;    dragon in slaughter perished.

Had this prodigy    by courage ensured

that he ring-hoard    ransack might

895    at his pleasure;    sea-boat loaded,

bore in bosom of ship    bright trappings,

Wæls's son;    snake hot melted.

He was of heroes    widely most famous

among nations,    warriors' shield,

900    for courage-deeds    —he by this had prospered—

since Heremod's    heroism ceased,

strength and spirit.    Heremod among Jutes was

into foes' power    forth betrayed,

swiftly despatched.    Him sorrow-surges

905    lamed too long;    he to his people grew,

to all followers    a living sorrow;

also often mourned    in earlier times

strong king's departure    wise men many,

who him for miseries'    amends had trusted.

910    that that prince's son    prosper should,

father's rank assume,    folk rule,

hoard and stronghold,    heroes' kingdom,

homeland of Scyldings.    Beowulf to all became,

孤身进入山洞,建下那桩奇功。

890 　他的宝剑刺穿巨大的长虫,
　　　闪光的武器深深扎进它背后的石壁;
　　　毒龙在这致命一击下一命呜呼。
　　　伟大的战士凭借自己的勇气
　　　如愿以偿,获得大宗宝藏。

895 　威尔斯之子把这些金银财宝
　　　搬上他的小船,装进船舱;
　　　那毒龙则在烈火中化为乌有。
　　　在远远近近所有部落中,
　　　西格蒙德堪称最著名的英雄——

900 　自从海勒摩德①失去英雄本色,　　　　　　① 丹麦国王,
　　　一蹶不振,他的声名便与日俱增,　　　　　暴君。
　　　成为武士的保护人。而海勒摩德
　　　则被朱特人出卖给他的仇敌,
　　　很快丢了性命。相反,西格蒙德

905 　历经千辛万苦,他的人民,
　　　他的追随者始终牵挂着他,
　　　许多智者曾经为他痛哭流涕,
　　　为这位勇士的离去而悲伤——
　　　他们期望他救黎民于水火——

910 　希望这位王子一帆风顺,
　　　继承他父亲的王位,保护百姓,
　　　包括他们的财产和城堡,
　　　保卫英雄之国,希尔德子孙的家园。

kinsman of Hygelac,    to mankind,

915    to friends more favouring;    Heremod violence consumed.

At times fleeting    fallow tracks

on steeds they sped.    Then was morning-light

shifted and scurried.    Went soldier many

determined    to hall the high

920    strange-wonder to see;    so too himself king

from bride-bower,    ring-hoards' guard,

stepped splendid    with stalwarts many,

for qualities quoted,    and his queen with him

mead-path paced    with maidens' company.


925    Hrothgar spoke,    he to hall went,

stood on step,    saw steep roof

with gold adorned    and Grendel's hand;

"For this sight    to Almighty thanks

swiftly be made!    Much I spite suffered,

930    griefs from Grendel;    ever may God work

wonder upon wonder,    glory's Keeper.

It was not long ago    that I any for me

for woes not hoped    in whole life

amends to meet,    when with blood mottled

935    house most splendid    sword-gory stood,

woe widespread    for wise men all,

those who not hoped    that they ever

故事唱完,海格拉克的亲属

915 　让人更觉亲切;海勒摩德则罪孽深重。
　　他们继续扬鞭策马,奔驰在
　　沙子路上。这时,东方的太阳
　　已经高高升起。许多勇敢的武士
　　涌入雄伟的大厅,争着观看

920 　这桩奇迹。赫罗斯加国王——
　　财宝的保护人也从寝宫出来,
　　威仪显赫地来到宴乐大厅,
　　一班壮士簇拥在国王左右,
　　王后陪同在他身边,周围跟着一班侍女。


925 　赫罗斯加进来后站在台阶上,
　　抬头望着金碧辉煌的屋顶,
　　发现了格兰道尔的手臂,他说:
　　"为了眼前这景象,我要感谢
　　全知全能的主! 这该死的格兰道尔

930 　让我吃足了苦头;但上帝——
　　光荣的庇护者从奇迹中再创奇迹。
　　不久以前,当这座美丽的大厅
　　被血腥的屠杀折腾得污秽不堪,
　　我的谋臣,我手下的每一个人

935 　都伤心绝望,我自己确实不敢奢望
　　有朝一日能摆脱这样的悲伤,
　　因为没有人觉得谁有足够的力量

nation's stronghold     from foes could protect,

from demons and devils.     Now warrior has

940     through Lord's power     deed performed,

which we all     before not might

by schemes contrive.     What! that may say

whichever woman     the man bore

among mankind,     if she yet lives,

945     that to her Old-ruler     gracious was

in child-bearing.     Now I, Beowulf, you,

man best,     for me like son will

love in life;     keep henceforth well

new kinship.     Not will be for you any lack

950     of worldly wishes,     if I my way have.

Very often I for less     rewards have granted,

hoard-honour     to humbier man,

inferior at fighting.     You for yourself have

by deeds ensured     that your fame lives

955     always for ever.     May Almighty you

with good reward,     as "he just now did."

Beowulf spoke,     son of Ecgtheow;

"We the brave-deed     with good-will great

to fight endeavoured,     boldly engaged

960     strength of unknown foe.     Would I rather

that you himself     to see were able,

foe in full array,     weary in death.

保卫这座人民的堡垒,使它免遭

仇敌的侵犯,免遭妖魔的蹂躏。

940　而今凭借上帝的伟力,一位勇士

完成了我们原先千方百计

无法完成的伟业。不错,不管哪位母亲,

生下这样的儿子——只要她还活着——

就可以说,全知全能的上帝

945　在她怀胎生育时特别恩宠。

噢,贝奥武甫,我的大英雄,

在我有生之年,我要把你当作

自己的儿子来爱护。请接受

这份亲情吧! 凡是我所有的,

950　都可以奖赏给你,让你得到满足。

平时我对下属创建的小小功勋

都慷慨地给予种种奖赏;

你用自己的壮举得到保证:

你的荣耀值得永世长存。

955　愿万能的上帝像以往那样

给予你最美好的回报吧。"

艾克塞奥之子贝奥武甫说:

"这一场战斗,我们打得很坚决,

大家奋不顾身,向一种未知的力量

960　发动勇敢的挑战。我真希望

你当时在场,能亲眼见证

你的仇敌如何死亡。要不是

I him quickly        in hard clasp

on fatal-bed        to fetter intended,

965    so that he in hand-grip        of mine should

lie life-struggling,        lest his body vanish;

I him not could,        when Ruler not wished,

from escaping stop,        nor I him so firmly held,

life-enemy;        was too very strong

970    foe in motion.        Yet he his hand left

as life-pledge        behind remaining,

arm and shoulder;        not with it any though

wretched creature        respite bought;

not the longer lives        loathed-wrecker

975    by sins ensnared,        but him wound has

in dread-grip        narrowly enclosed,

in fatal fetters;        there await shall

creature crime-stained        mighty judgement,

how him bright Ruler        punish will."

980        Then was less wordy man,        son of Ecglaf,

in boast-speech        of war-actions,

when noble men        by earl's strength

above high roof        hand observed,

fiend's fingers;        at front each was

985    of sockets nails        steel most-like,

heathen's hand-claw,        battle-creature's

talon terrible;        everyone said

被他脱身,我真恨不得

用我的铁腕把他牢牢捆绑,

965 　按在灵床上,让他在我的掌握中

为了活命而苦苦地挣扎。

我没能阻止他逃走,因为

主不愿意我这样做;而且,

我也抓得不够紧,那仇敌

970 　有的是蛮力。不过,为了逃命,

他已把自己的手臂和肩膀留下

作为侵犯鹿厅的证据。可恶的魔怪

即便逃走也得不到安慰,

凶狠的掠夺者罪孽深重,

975 　已活不了多久,因为他受的伤

不是太轻,足以要他的性命。

就像一个犯罪的不法之徒,

他在等待严正的判决,光荣的主

不久将颁布对他的惩处。"

980 　恶魔的爪子高高挂在屋顶上,

众贵胄一个个抬头观看,

喜欢自吹自擂的艾格拉夫之子①

这时变成了哑巴,一言不发。

恶魔的指尖——那一个个指甲

985 　钢铁般坚硬;异教徒的手指

实际上充当了魔鬼的钉耙!

人人都说这样一个怪物,

① 即曾经嘲笑过贝奥武甫的安佛斯。

that him hard-fighters' no    hurt would

iron old and trusty,    that none the monster's

990    bloody battle-arm    injure would.


Then was ordered quickly    Heorot within

by hands adorned;    many there were

of men and women    who the wine-house

guest-hall made ready.    Gold-bright shone

995    weaving along walls,    wonder-sights many

for people all    who on such things stare.

Was that bright building    broken badly,

all interior    with iron-bonds secure,

hinges unsprung;    roof alone escaped

1000    entirely sound,    when the monster

of grim-deeds guilty    in flight turned,

of life despairing.    Not death easy is

to flee from    —try he who will—

but seek he must    soul-bearers',

1005    by need compelled,    men's sons',

earth-dwellers'    prepared place,

where his body,    in death-bed secure,

sleeps after feasting.    Then was time and hour

that to hall went    Halfdane's son;

1010    wished himself king    feast partake.

Not heard I the tribe    in greater force

任何铁器对他都无可奈何，

恶魔那双沾满鲜血的手，

990　　能予以伤害的利刃亘古未有。


国王随后颁布命令，要人们

将鹿厅装饰一新。男男女女

开始布置宴乐和迎宾的大殿。

墙上的装饰金光闪耀，许许多多

995　　奇妙的景象出现在人们眼前。

尽管这座大厦金碧辉煌，内部

有许多铁环扣紧，但它还是遭到

严重的损坏。门上的铰链

都已脱落，只有整个屋顶

1000　完好无损，因为当时那恶魔——

尽管作恶多端——已经陷入绝境，

只顾着逃命。不过，躲避死亡

并非易事——谁不信就试试——

一个人命中注定得寻找归宿，

1005　那是专为大地的居民，灵魂的负荷者，

人类的子孙备下的住所，

人生的宴席一旦结束，人的躯壳

就得在自己的灵床上长眠。

哈夫丹之子准时进入大厅，

1010　国王要亲自参加这次盛宴。

我从未听说哪个部落有这么多人

about their treasure-giver      better faring.

Bent then to bench     fame-wielders,

at feast rejoiced;     fittingly received

1015   mead-cups many;     kinsmen were

stout-hearted    in hall the high,

Hrothgar and Hrothulf.    Heorot inside was

with friends filled;    no traitor-deeds

Folk-Scyldings    as yet transacted.

1020     Gave then to Beowulf    son of Halfdane

standard golden    as victory's reward,

braided battle-banner,    helm and byrnie;

splendid treasure-sword    many saw

before hero brought.    Beowulf took

1025   flagon on hall-floor;    not he of the fee-gift

before sharp-shooters    ashamed need be.

Not heard I friendlier    four treasures

with gold adorned    men many

on ale-bench    to others giving.

1030   Around that helmet's roof    head-guard

with wires encircled    rim outside protected,

so that him filed sword    savagely not might

battle-hard scathe,    when shield-fighter

against enemies    go forth should.

1035     Ordered then earls' defender    eight horses

with gold head-gear    on hall-floor led

簇拥在财宝的赐予者身边。

勇敢的战士一个个兴高采烈，

在长凳上就座。雄伟的大厅里，

1015　赫罗斯加国王和赫罗索夫①

应酬自如，频频举杯畅饮。

宴乐厅挤满了四方来宾：

当时的希尔德子孙预料不到

后来叛逆的阴谋能够得逞。②

1020　作为胜利的嘉奖，哈夫丹之子

赠给贝奥武甫一面描金的战旗，

一个头盔和一副护胸甲。

许多人还看见一把珍贵的宝剑

送到英雄手里。贝奥武甫

1025　当众喝下一盅酒。在勇士面前，

他无须为接受这份厚礼而汗颜。

我从未听说有谁在宴会上

如此友好地向另一个人

赠送如此珍贵的四件宝物。

1030　那头盔顶端有一个盔冠，

它用钢丝扎成，作为护饰，

戴上这样的头盔，勇敢的战士

如果上战场与仇敌厮杀，

锋利的刀刃再也伤害不了他。

1035　百姓的庇护者又传下命令，

将八匹披着金辔的骏马牵进

① 赫罗斯加的侄子。

② 赫罗斯加死后，赫罗索夫曾发动叛乱，篡夺王位。

in under ramparts: of them on one stood

saddle skilfully adorned, with iewels decorated;

it was battle-seat of high-king,

1040 when in swords' play son of Halfdane

join wished; never in vanguard failed

far-famed's war-skill when the slain were falling.

And then to Beowulf of both gifts

protector of Ing's friends possession gave,

1045 horses and weapons; told him well enjoy.

Thus in manly fashion famed chieftain.

hoard-guard of heroes for battle-clashes paid

in horses and treasures, so them never one could fault,

he who tell will truth as well as right.


1050 Still to each one of earls' band,

those who with Beowulf brine-path travelled,

on the mead-bench treasures he gave,

heirlooms, and the one man decreed

in gold to be atoned, whom Grendel first

1055 in malice killed, as he of them more would,

save for them wise God that fate prevented

and this man's courage. Ruler all controlled

for human kind, as he now still does.

And so is prudence everywhere the best,

1060 mind's forethought. Much shall suffer

宴乐大厅。其中一匹的马鞍上

珠宝琳琅满目,装饰得格外漂亮。

这马原来是国王自己的坐骑,

1040 想当年,哈夫丹之子就骑着它

冲杀在战场上。即使尸横遍野,

声名显赫的国王也从不停鞭歇马。

英格①子民的保护者把这名驹,

连同马鞍,送给了贝奥武甫,

1045 并嘱咐他好好享用这两件宝物。

就这样,著名的国王,财产的保护人

用良马和珍宝慷慨地酬谢了

勇士的丰功伟绩——说句实话,

这样的做法论礼节已够到家。


1050 国王然后又向那些与贝奥武甫

一道渡海而来的武士赠送礼物

和传世的珍宝;他还下令

献上一笔黄金,作为那位

被格兰道尔残害的勇士的补偿——

1055 如果没有智慧的上帝庇护,

没有贝奥武甫的勇敢,格兰道尔

一定会把更多的生命摧残。

创世主一如既往掌握着

人类的命运。因此,时时处处

1060 你都得小心谨慎,深谋远虑。

① 传说中的丹麦国王。

91

good and evil he who for long here

in these strife-days world enjoys.

 There was song and music strung together

before Halfdane's battle-leader,

1065 glee-wood strummed, tale often told,

when hall-joy Hrothgar's bard

along mead-bench utter should,

about Finn's heirs. When them the onslaught hit,

hero of Half-Danes, Hnæf the Scylding,

1070 on Frisian field to fall was fated.

 Not however Hildeburh to praise had need

Jutes' loyalty; guiltless she was

bereft of loved ones in the shield-play,

bairn and brother; they in doom fell,

1075 by spear wounded; that was unhappy woman.

Not without cause Hoc's daughter

fate's verdict mourned, when morning came,

then she under sky see could

slaughter of kinsmen, where she before most held

1080 worldly joy. War all destroyed

Finn's thanes except few only,

so that he not might in that meeting-place

the clash with Hengest at all conclude,

nor the woeful remnant by war remove,

1085 prince's thane; but they them peace-terms offered,

人生艰难,只要你活在世上,

就难免遭遇种种离合悲欢。

这时,歌乐之声响起,吟游诗人

当着哈夫丹之子赫罗斯加的面

1065 拨动琴弦,讲述故事,为宴乐厅

带来欢乐的消遣。这一次

他叙述的是芬恩①部属的事迹, ① 朱特部落的
酋长。

当灾难突然降临在他们身上,

丹麦人的英雄赫纳夫②,命中注定 ② 丹麦部落的
酋长。

1070 在弗罗西亚的战场上丧命。

希德贝尔③没有必要称赞 ③ 丹麦王霍
克之女,赫纳夫

朱特人的信义:她并无过错 的亲姐姐,芬恩

但战争使她失去自己的亲人—— 之妻。

儿子和兄弟,他们的死亡

1075 由命运决定;好一个不幸的女子!

霍克的女儿并非无缘无故

哀叹残酷的命运,因为第二天一早

她亲眼看见自己的亲人被杀害——

在这之前,她享尽了人间幸福。

1080 一场血战使芬恩的部属

损失大半,幸存者寥寥无几,因此

他没有力量与亨格斯特④ ④ 赫纳夫手下
将领。

继续较量,没有能力赶走

国王的部将,以保护幸存者的性命。

1085 他们于是提出和平条件:

that they for them other hearth     entirely cleared,

hall and high-seat,     that they of-half control

with Jutes' sons     have might,

and with fee-gifts     Folcwalda's son

1090     day every     Danes should honour,

Hengest's band     with rings should treat,

with even as much     treasure-store

of ornate gold     as he Frisian tribe

in beer-hall     embolden would.

1095     Then they confirmed     on both sides

firm peace-treaty.     Finn to Hengest

with courage undisputed     oaths declared,

that he the woeful remnant     by wise men's judgement

in honour would hold,     so that there any man

1100     by words nor deeds     treaty not should break,

nor through cunning     ever complain,

though they their ring-giver's     killer followed,

lordless,     when on them thus forced it was;

if then Frisian any     by hostile speech

1105     of the murder-hate     reminding was,

then it sword's edge     settle should.

    Pyre was prepared,     and homely gold

fetched from hoard.     War-Scyldings'

best battle-man     was on pyre ready.

1110     At the pyre was     easy-seen

给丹麦人腾出另外一座大厦，

里面有厅堂和宝座，让他们

与朱特人的子孙一起，各自占领

宫廷的一半。福克华尔德之子①    ① 即芬恩。

1090   还必须每天犒赏丹麦人，

向亨格斯特手下将士赠送

金银财宝，就像他以往

在雄伟的宴乐厅犒赏

他的弗罗西亚同胞那样。

1095   双方做出保证，和平条约

就此签订。芬恩向亨格斯特

立下誓言，说他将遵照谋臣的裁断，

尊重战争中幸存的丹麦人，

保证任何人不得以语言和行动

1100   破坏和约，任何人不得恶意诽谤，

说丹麦人失去了自己的国王，

如今只是出于无奈，才追随

杀死了他们的主公的凶犯。

如果有哪位弗罗西亚人不怀好意，

1105   坚持要将血腥的仇恨唤起，

那就用剑刀把他的嘴封住。

葬礼准备就绪，闪光的金子

从仓库搬出。丹麦杰出的武士

抬上了柴堆。人们不难看见

1110   柴堆上堆着许多盔甲，一件件

blood-stained sark,    swine all-golden,

boar iron-hard,    hero many

by wounds destroyed;    great men in slaughter fell.

Ordered then Hildeburh    at Hnæf's pyre

1115    her own son    to flame consigned,

bone-house burned,    and in fire placed

by uncle's shoulder.    Woman mourned,

sorrowed with songs.    Warrior was laid aloft.

Soared into clouds    slain-fire hugest,

1120    roared before mound;    heads melted,

wound-gates burst    when blood gushed out,

hate-bites of body.    Blaze all swallowed,

guest greediest,    those who there battle took

from both peoples;    was their power departed.


1125    Returned then fighters    hearths to seek,

of friends bereft,    Frisia to see,

homes and high-fort.    Hengest still

slaughter-stained winter    spent with Finn

all distraught;    land he remembered,

1130    though he not could    on sea drive

ring-prowed ship;    sea in storm surged,

wrestled with wind,    winter waves locked

in icy bonds,    until other came

year in dwellings,    as now still it does,

血迹斑斑,上面野猪的徽章

闪闪发光——那么多人重伤而亡,

那么多人在血战中毙命。

希德贝尔然后吩咐下属

1115 把她儿子的尸体也抬上柴堆,

与他的舅父赫纳夫并排,

一道进行焚化。王后悲悲戚戚,

哀声歌唱。武士的尸体高居在

柴堆之上。死亡的火焰在山丘上

1120 咆哮着直冲云天。头颅一个个

开始熔化,由于伤口绽开,

血珠四下飞溅。火焰——那贪婪的精灵

吞噬着一切,吞噬了双方的阵亡者,

他们的勇力从此化为乌有。

1125 失去伙伴的武士然后返回居地

去守护自己的家园和城堡。

亨格斯特则与芬恩待在一起,

他念念不忘那场屠杀,孤独地

度过一个冬天。他怀念自己的家乡,

1130 但又不能驾驶镶金的帆船

渡过海洋;海上暴雨阵阵,

狂风呼啸,严寒用冰雪将海水封锁,

直到新的一年来到人间。

时序交替——至今也是如此,

1135   those which always     seasons observe,

glory-bright weathers.    Then was winter gone,

fair was earth's breast;    yearned the exile,

guest, from dwellings;    he of grief-revenge

sooner thought    than of sea-path,

1140   and if he strife-clash    contrive might,

so that he Jutes' sons    with iron could remind.

So he not denied    world's counsel

when him Hunlaf's son    battle-gleaming

blade finest    in lap placed;

1145   its were among Jutes    edges known.

    So too deadly foe's    Finn in turn received

sword-onslaught cruel    at his own home,

when fierce assault    Gudlaf and Oslaf

after sea-journey    sorrow bemoaned,

1150   blamed woes' tally;    not might restless spirit

be restrained in heart.    Then was hall reddened

with foes' lives,    so too Finn slain,

king in company,    and the queen seized.

Sharp-shooters of Scyldings    to ships ferried

1155   all house-goods    of nation-king

which they in Finn's home    find were able

jewels, treasure-gems.    They on sea-path

noble lady    to Danes ferried,

led to people.    Song was sung,

1135　天气转暖，一切都按季节

　　　　有序地运行。冬天已经过去，

　　　　大地的胸怀一片烂漫，流亡者急欲

　　　　返回家乡：但他更渴望复仇，

　　　　而不是航海，只要他能够

1140　挑起一场战争，他就可以用刀枪

　　　　让朱特人的子孙把血债清算。

　　　　因此，当亨拉夫之子把他那把

　　　　闪闪发光的宝剑——朱特人

　　　　十分熟悉的刀刃搁在他的膝盖上，①

1145　他没有拒绝世俗的惯例。

　　　　就这样，残忍的杀戮反过来落到

　　　　勇敢的芬恩头上——他自己的家

　　　　成了屠杀场。当古德拉夫和奥斯拉夫②

　　　　渡过大海，抱怨那场屠杀和伤害，

1150　并痛斥造成不幸的元凶：

　　　　不平静的心就再难约束。

　　　　宫廷于是被鲜血染红，芬恩

　　　　及其部下被杀，王后被掳。

　　　　丹麦人的武士把国王的财富，

1155　包括项链和各种宝石珍玩——

　　　　凡是在芬恩家里能找到的——

　　　　全部装船运走。他们把高贵的夫人

　　　　从海上带回丹麦，回到她自己的部落。

　　　　吟游诗人的歌已经唱完，

① 亨拉夫死于朱特人之手，其子把死者的宝剑放在亨格斯特的膝盖上，请求他为他父亲报仇。　② 两者为亨拉夫的兄弟。

1160    glee-man's tale.    Joy again sprang up,

boomed out bench-noise,    cup-bearers served

wine from wondrous vessels.    Then came Wealhtheow forth

walking in golden neck-ring    to where the good two

sat, uncle and nephew;    still was their kinship together,

1165    each to the other true.    Also there Unferth spokesman

at feet sat of lord of Scyldings;    each his life trusted,

that he had courage great,    though he to his kin was not

honour-firm in edges' clashes.    Spoke then lady of Scyldings:

"Receive this cup,    noble lord of mine,

1170    treasure-giver.    You joyful were,

gold-friend of men,    and to Geats spoke

gentle words,    as ought a man to do.

Be to Geats gracious,    of gifts mindful,

which from near and far    you now possess.

1175    To me one said    that you for son wished

this warrior to have.    Heorot is cleansed,

ring-hall brilliant;    enjoy while you may

many rewards,    and to your kinsmen leave

folk and kingdom    when you forth must go,

1180    fated-death see.    I my know

gracious Hrothulf,    that he the youths will

in honour hold,    if you earlier than he,

friend of Scyldings,    world leave;

think I that he with good    repay will

1160　欢乐的气氛再次高涨,人声喧闹,

　　　沸沸扬扬,侍者们从精制的壶中

　　　倒出玉液琼浆。王后维瑟欧

　　　脖子上挂着金项链,款款来到

　　　叔侄两人跟前:当时他们尚未反目,

1165　相互仍以诚相待。能言善辩的安佛斯

　　　也坐在国王身旁:尽管他在争斗中

　　　有愧于自己的兄弟,但大家仍相信

　　　他具有非凡的勇气。王后开口说:

　　　"请喝下这杯酒,我的夫君,

1170　财富的赐予者,愿你心情愉快,

　　　武士的挚友,请你尽自己的责任

　　　把最美好的祝福献给高特人。

　　　请你宽厚待人,你有许许多多

　　　来自四方的礼品,别忘了奖赏他们。

1175　有人还告诉我,你有意把那位勇士

　　　收为义子。如今金碧辉煌的宴乐厅

　　　已经打扫干净。请慷慨地颁发

　　　各种奖赏吧,直到你升遐作古,

　　　遵照主的旨意离开人间,那时

1180　再把你的亲人和王国留下。

　　　我知道,如果你——丹麦人的朋友

　　　先一步弃世而去,仁慈的赫罗索夫

　　　将会忠心辅佐你的年轻武士①。　　　① 指他们的

　　　我相信,只要他没有忘记　　　儿子。

1185   our children,     if he it all remembers,

what we for his happiness    and for his honour

in his youth before    favours bestowed."

     Turned then by bench,    where her boys were,

Hrethric and Hrothmund,    and heroes' sons,

1190   youth-band together;    there the good sat

Beowulf of Geats    by the brothers two.


     Him was cup brought,    and friendship

in words lavished,    and twisted gold

kindly offered,    arm-ornaments two,

1195   robe and rings,    necklet largest

of those which I on earth    heard of have.

None I under sky    better heard

from hoard-treasures of heroes,    since Hama bore off

to the shining stronghold    Brosings' necklet,

1200   jewel and casket;    trick-hates he fled

of Eormenric,    chose eternal gain.

     That ring had    Hygelac of Geats,

grandson of Swerting,    on last campaign,

when he under banner    riches guarded,

1205   slaughter-loot defended;    him fate took off,

when he through pride    disaster courted,

feud with Frisians.    He the jewel wore,

exotic stones    over waves' beaker,

1185 　在他孩提时我们如何宠爱他，

　　　如何使他获得幸福和荣耀，

　　　他一定会忠心回报我们的孩子。"

　　　王后然后转身朝向她的两个儿子——

　　　赫里斯雷克和赫罗斯蒙德，

1190 　以及那一大群年轻武士，两兄弟中间

　　　坐着高特人的英雄贝奥武甫。


　　　王后把酒杯端到他面前，

　　　用友好的言辞向他表示敬意，

　　　并彬彬有礼地向他赠送

1195 　金镯、盔饰、战袍、戒指，以及

　　　一只世上绝无仅有的大项圈。

　　　普天之下，我从未听说有什么宝贝

　　　能比布罗辛的项圈更其珍贵，

　　　它原由哈马连同宝盒带到

1200 　光明之城：他逃脱了爱曼里克

　　　险恶的阴谋，得到了永久的特权。①

　　　高特国王海格拉克——斯华丁之孙

　　　在他最后一次历险中将这项圈

　　　戴在身上，②在战旗下保卫战争中

1205 　掠得的财富。然而，当他耀武扬威

　　　向弗罗西亚人挑衅，命运之神

　　　却掳走了他。强大的国王

　　　携带那件宝物跨过海洋，

① 布罗辛的项圈据传为女神弗雷娅的宝物。哈马事迹不详，似乎是他从东哥特王国国王爱曼里克那里把宝物偷出，带到了丹麦。

② 贝奥武甫回国后将项圈献给了国王海格拉克，这里叙述的故事发生在海格拉克得到项圈后。

powerful chieftain;    he under shield fell.

1210    Passed then into Franks' grasp    body of king,

breast-armour,    and the ring together;

worse war-fighters    the slain plundered

after battle-carnage;    Geats' bodies

corpse-field filled.    Hall with noise resounded.

1215    Wealhtheow spoke,    she before the retinue said:

"Enjoy this ring,    Beowulf, beloved

warrior, with good luck,    and this robe use,

nation's treasure,    and thrive well,

prove yourself by strength,    and to these lads be

1220    in counsels kind.    I you its reward will give.

Have you achieved    that you far and near

all and forever    men will praise,

even as widely    as sea surrounds,

wind-yard, cliff-walls.    Be while you live,

1225    lordly man, happy!    I you wish well

of treasure-riches.    Be you to sons of mine

in deeds indulgent,    joy-possessing!

Here is every man    to other true,

in mind merciful,    to liege-lord loyal;

1230    thanes are united,    nation all alert,

drink-cheered retinue    does as I bid."

Went then to seat.    There was feast finest,

drank wine men.    Fate not they knew,

结果倒毙在自己的盾下。

1210　他的尸体落到法兰克人手里，
　　　连同盔甲和那个硕大的项圈。
　　　血战结束，平庸的武士搜劫死者，
　　　战场上到处是高特人的尸体。
　　　宴乐厅再次响起一片欢呼。

1215　维瑟欧当着众人的面说：
　　　"收下这个项圈吧，亲爱的贝奥武甫，
　　　祝你好运，年轻人，享用这套盔甲。
　　　它是我国的宝物，愿你万事如意；
　　　让你的勇力四海传扬，并请费心

1220　教导这两个孩子：我会重重赏你。
　　　你已创下功勋，无论什么地方
　　　人们都将永远把你的事迹颂扬，
　　　你的英名将像大海——风的家园
　　　那样广阔无边。高贵的王子，

1225　愿你在这里生活幸福！我希望
　　　你能对这些宝物感到满意。有福的人，
　　　请你宽厚地对待我的儿子！
　　　我们这里每个人都很真诚，
　　　都很善良，都忠于自己的国王。

1230　大臣们团结一致，全国众志成城，
　　　扈从们性格开朗，听从我的召唤。"
　　　王后回到自己的座位。宴席真够丰盛，
　　　男人们开怀畅饮。他们不知道

old destiny grim,     as it happened had

1235  to heroes many.    Then evening came,

and Hrothgar went    to quarters his,

ruler to rest.    Hall guarded

host of men,    as they often had done.

Bench-wood they bared;    it through-spread was

1240  with bedding and bolsters.    Beer-warrior one,

death-near and doomed,    in hall-bed lay down.

They set at their heads    battle-shields,

board-woods bright;    there on bench was

over each fine man    clearly seen

1245  battle-steep helmet,    ringed byrnie,

spear-shaft sturdy.    Was custom their

that they often were    for war prepared

both at home and out harrying,    and either of these,

just such times    as for their liege-lord

1250  need arose;    was the nation worthy.

当夜幕降临,赫罗斯加返回

1235　寝宫安歇,那严酷的命运

又将落到他们身上,就像以往

出现过的那样。一大班勇士

一如既往,留下保卫宴乐大厅。

他们把凳子搬过一边,在地板上

1240　铺设床枕。其中一个武士

命中该绝,躺下后就呼呼大睡。

他们将闪闪发光的盾牌

搁在枕边;人们不难看见

他们身旁的长凳上堆放着

1245　历经百战的头盔、带环的胸甲,以及

坚固的长矛。他们养成了习惯:

随时准备战斗,不管那战场

在家里还是在旷野,无论何时何故,

他们都听从国王的吩咐,

1250　丹麦不愧为一个伟大的民族!

# PART SIX
## Grendel's Mother's Attack

Sank then to sleep.     One sorely paid for

evening rest,     as to them very often happened,

since gold-hall     Grendel guarded,

evil inflicted,     until the end arrived,

1255  death for sins.     That clear became,

wide-known to men,     that an avenger still

lived after the loathed one,     for a long time,

after war-grief;     Grendel's mother.

mistress monster-woman     misery remembered,

1260  she who water-horror     inhabit must,

cold currents,     since Cain became

the sword-slayer     of his only brother,

father's son;     he then doomed departed,

by murder marked     man's joy to flee,

1265  wasteland settled.     Thence sprang many

fateful spirits;     was of them Grendel one,

sword-exile hateful,     who at Heorot found

watching warrior     for war waiting;

there with him monster     to grips got;

1270  yet he remembered     might's strength,

# 六
# 格兰道尔母亲的袭击

他们于是进入梦乡,其中一位
却为这一觉付出惨重的代价,
就像先前格兰道尔霸占宴乐厅,
末日与死亡随即降临那样。

1255　人们很快发现,真相终于大白:
经过那场惨烈的生死争战,
仍有一位复仇者活在世上。
格兰道尔的母亲,那个妖妇,
那个恶魔,念念不忘她的悲伤,

1260　自从该隐杀害了自己的兄弟——
父亲的儿子,她就只得居住在
可怕的水府,寒冷的水乡,
由于那桩罪恶,她命中注定
被剥夺人世间的幸福生活,

1265　被流放于荒野。从她那里滋生出诸多
妖魔鬼怪,格兰道尔即这样一位
可恶的流放者,他在鹿厅发现
一位守夜者等待着与他交战。
恶魔一把抓住了他,然而,

1270　守夜者没有忘记运用自己的神力,

generous gift,     which him God gave,

and to One-ruler's     favour trusted,

comfort and help;     by this he the foe defeated,

laid low hell's spirit.     Then he wretched went,

1275 of joy deprived,     death-place to see,

mankind's foe.     And his mother still

greedy and gloom-hearted     go forth would

with sorrowing step,     son's death to avenge.

     Came then to Heorot,     where Ring-Danes

1280 through the hall slept.     Then there at once was

setback for soldiers,     when inside stole

Grendel's mother.     Was the horror less

by just as much     as is female strength,

war-power of woman,     compared with weaponed man,

1285 when blade bound,     by hammer forged,

sword with blood stained     swine upon helmet

with edges tough     opposite shears.

     Then was in hall     hard-edged drawn

sword a bove seats,     broad shield many

1290 held in hand firm;     helmet not heeded,

byrnie broad,     when him the horror sighted.

     She was in haste,     wanted out thence,

life to save;     when she discovered was;

quickly she warrior     one had

1295 firmly seized,     then she to fen went back.

那是主慷慨赐予他的礼物,
他信赖万能的主,并由此
得到安慰和帮助。他凭此战胜仇敌,
制服了地狱的精灵。那人类的敌人

1275　只好落荒而走,伤心绝望地
去寻找自己的葬身地。而他的母亲,
那女妖既贪婪又凶狠,继续
铤而走险,决心为儿子报仇。
她于是来到鹿厅,丹麦人

1280　睡梦未醒。当格兰道尔之母
悄悄进门,不幸即刻落到
兵士身上。不过,这女妖的袭击
不像格兰道尔那样令人生畏,因为
女人的力气毕竟稍逊于

1285　全副武装的男子,战场上舞刀弄枪,
需要举起鲜血淋淋的刀剑
砍开对方头盔上野猪的盔饰。
丹麦的武士即刻从长凳上
拿起刀枪,将一面面圆盾

1290　提在手里:由于心怀恐惧,
竟忘了戴上头盔,穿上戎装。
女妖也慌慌张张,一旦被发现,
就急于脱身以保全自己的性命。
她迅速抓住一位武士,然后

1295　即刻返回她的沼泽地。

He was to Hrothgar      hero best-loved

in retinue's rank      between seas,

sturdy shield-warrior,      whom she from bed snatched,

glorious man.      Was not Beowulf there,

1300 but was other lodging      earlier assigned

after treasure-giving      to glorious Geat.

Uproar was in Heorot;      she in its gore seized

well-known arm;      care was renewed,

returned to dwellings.      Not was that bargain good,

1305 which they on both sides      buy must

with friends' lives.      Then was wise king.

hoary battle-man      in wretched heart,

when he lordly thane      unliving,

the dearest      dead knew.

1310      Quickly was to bower      Beowulf fetched,

victorious man.      At early-day

went warrior best,      noble champion,

self with companions      where the wise king waited,

whether for him Almighty      ever will

1315 after woeful news      a change achieve.

     Went then over floor      war-worthy man

with his hand-picked band,      hall-wood dinned,

that he the wise      in words addressed

lord of Ing's friends,      asked if for him was

1320 after pleasure-feast      night pleasing.

被抓走的是一位光荣的武士，
四海之内，在所有的扈从中
最受赫罗斯加国王的恩宠。
贝奥武甫当时没有在场：
1300　受奖以后，这位光荣的高特人
被安排在另一个处所休息。
鹿厅里喊声震天；血污的魔爪
也被女妖抢回。哀伤与焦虑
重新笼罩大厅。这不是一笔好交易，
1305　因为双方都失去了自己的亲戚。
当白发苍苍的老王得知
高贵的大臣，他最宠信的扈从
死于非命，好不伤心！
于是，战无不胜的贝奥武甫
1310　很快被国王请到宴乐厅。
这位杰出的战士，高贵的统帅，
与他的部下一道，一大早
就赶往鹿厅，老国王在那里
正等着他，想知道全能的主
1315　是否愿意将这种局面改变。
高贵的武士与他的随从
昂首进入大厅，脚下的地板
发出回响，他向英明的国王——
英格的朋友问候：昨天晚上
1320　他是否随心所愿，睡得很香？

Hrothgar spoke,      helm of Scyldings:

"Not ask you about pleasures!      Sorrow is renewed

for Danish nation.      Dead is Æschere,

Yrmenlaf's      elder brother,

1325    my confidant     and my counsellor,

shoulder companion,     when we in battle

head defended,     when clashed armies,

boar-helmets smashed.     Such should man be,

a noble old and trusty,     as Æschere was.

1330     Was to him in Heorot     hand-slayer

death-spirit errant;     I know not whither

terrible corpse-gloating     backways she went,

at feast delighted.     She the feud avenged

in which you yesternight     Grendel killed

1335    by violent means     in harsh embrace,

because he too long     natlon ot mine

diminished and destroyed.     He in fight fell

of life guilty,     and now other came

mighty crime-scather,     would her son avenge,

1340    and far has     feud upheld,

as it seem may     to thane many

who for treasure-giver     in breast weeps,

heart-grief hard;     now the hand lies low,

which you in all     desires supported.

丹麦人的庇护者赫罗斯加说:
"别向我问安了! 悲伤又笼罩
丹麦王国。叶曼拉夫的长兄
伊斯切尔昨晚死了,他是

1325 我的亲信,我的谋士,并肩
作战的伙伴,昔日我们一起
战场上相互照应,率领士兵
与头戴钢盔的敌人交战。
他是个大好人,永远值得信任。

1330 如今凶猛的精灵把他
杀害在鹿厅。我不知道这魔怪
带着她的猎物扬扬得意
去哪里用餐。她为报仇而来——
昨天晚上,你用自己的铁掌

1335 将格兰道尔置于死地,因为
他多年来一直残害、屠杀
我的子民。他在搏斗中败阵,
丢了性命,如今却来了另一位
作恶多端的罪犯,一心为

1340 她的儿子报仇,而且已经得手——
因为许多人心里都在流泪,
为失去财富的赐予者①而悲伤。
那双曾经如此有力地支持过
你的手,如今已无力地垂下。

① 伊斯切尔虽不是国王,但有自己的宴乐厅和扈从。

115

1345    I it land-dwellers,      people of mine,

hall-counsellors      tell have heard

that they saw      such two

massive march-steppers      moors haunting,

alien spirits.    Of them one was

1350    as they clearest      to discern were able,

of woman's likeness.      Other wretch-shaped

in man's form      exile-tracks trod,

but he was larger      than any man other;

him in yore-days      Grendel named

1355    earth-dwellers;    not they father know,

whether him any was      earlier born

of hidden spirits.    They secret land

inhabit wolf-slopes,      windy nesses,

wild fen-path,      where mountain stream

1360    under crags' shadows      downward dives,

flood under earth.    Not is that far hence

of mile-measure      that the mere stands;

over it hang      hoary groves,

tree by roots fixed      water overshadows.

1365    There one may on nights all      deadly wonder see,

fire on flood.    None enough wise lives

of men's sons      who the bottom knows.

    Though the heath-stepper,      by hounds harried,

hart with horns tough      forest seeks,

1345　我曾听我的同胞,我的人民,以及

　　　　大厅的谋士说,他们曾经在荒野

　　　　见过这两个身材魁梧的浪游者,

　　　　异族的精灵,出没在沼泽地。

　　　　他们还能够清楚地辨别

1350　其中一位看上去像个女子。

　　　　另外一位外貌丑陋,外表像个男子,

　　　　踏着流放者疲惫的脚步,

　　　　只是身躯特别高大。

　　　　当地人一直管他叫格兰道尔,

1355　但不知道他的父亲是谁,

　　　　更不知在他们以前还有

　　　　别的什么孽障。他们占据着

　　　　神秘的疆土,野狼的坡地,

　　　　迎风的山岬,险恶的沼泽,

1360　那里有山水直泻黑暗的深渊,

　　　　形成地下的洪流。离这里不远,

　　　　仅数里之遥,就有一个深潭,

　　　　它的四周是一片结着冰霜的树林,

　　　　古木盘根错节,悬在水面上。

1365　每天晚上,可以看见一个奇景:

　　　　洪流上冒出火光。人类的子孙,

　　　　不管见识多广,都不知这潭有多深。

　　　　任何长角的雄鹿,即使被猎狗

　　　　紧紧追赶,长途奔命后进入树林,

1370    from far pursued,     first he life gives up,

breath on bank,     before he in will leap

head to save;    not is it pleasant place.

Thence wave-swirl    up mounts

dark to clouds,    when wind stirs

1375    dreadful storms,    until sky glowers,

heavens weep.    Now the remedy belongs

again to you alone.    Region yet not you know,

ghastly place    where you find might

criminal creature;    seek if you dare.

1380    I you the feud    with wealth reward,

with ancient treasures    as I earlier did,

with twisted gold    if you away come."


    Beowulf spoke,    son of Ecgtheow:

      "Not sorrow,wise man!    Better is for everyone

1385    that he his friend avenge,    than he much mourn.

Of us each must    end abide

in world of life;    achieve he who may

glory before death;    that is for warrior

unliving    afterwards best.

1390     Arise, kingdom's guardian,    let us quickly go,

Grendel's kin's    spoor to scan.

I it you swear:    not she in cover will be lost,

nor in earth's embrace,    nor in mountain wood,

1370 宁可将性命丧失在堤岸上，
也不愿跃入潭中寻求庇护。
那里的确不是一个好处所！
当狂风卷起可怕的暴雨，
潭中便浊浪翻腾，黑雾直升云端，

1375 直到天空变得阴阴沉沉，大地
恸哭失声！如今补救的责任
再次落到你一人身上。不过，
你现在仍不知罪犯的藏身之地；
如果你有胆量，可以找到那里。

1380 只要你活着出来，我定会
重重赏你，就像上次我拿出
奇珍异宝和项圈奖赏你那样。"


艾克塞奥之子贝奥武甫说：
"请不必悲伤，智慧的国王！

1385 与其哀悼朋友，不如为他报仇。
人生在世，谁都不免一死，
要死就让他死得轰轰烈烈，
对于武士来说，那样的死
才是人生最美好的事。

1390 动身吧，王国的保护人，让我们
马上出发去探寻妖母的行踪，
我向你保证，不管她逃到哪里，
无论她钻入地下，还是躲进深山，

nor in ocean's depth,     go where she will.

1395    This day you     patience have

in miseries all,     as I you expect to."

    Leapt up then the old king,     God thanked,

mighty Lord,     for what the man spoke.

    Then was for Hrothgar     horse bridled,

1400    mount with braided mane.     Wise chieftain

splendid rode;     foot-troop marched

of shield-bearers.     Tracks were

along wood-swathes     widely seen,

trail over grounds,     where she forwards fared

1405    over murky moor,     of kin-thanes she carried

the finest,     soul-less,

of those who with Hrothgar     home defended.

    Over-went then     heroes' son

steep stone slopes,     foot-ways narrow,

1410    cramped single-paths,     unknown course,

towering crags,     monster-lairs many;

he with few     ahead went

wise men     terrain scanning,

until he all at once     mountain trees

1415    over hoary stone     hanging found,

joyless forest;     water below stood

bloody and disturbed.     For Danes all was,

for friends of Scyldings     pain at heart

抑或潜入海底,都要把她找出来。

1395 今天,请你暂且克制悲伤——

这是我对你的唯一期望。"

老国王站起身,因勇士的一番话

感谢天上的主,万能的上帝。

于是,一匹长鬃名驹作为国王的坐骑

1400 给安上了鞍辔。英明的领袖,

扬鞭策马,持盾的军士跟随他

步行前进。那妖母的足迹

清晰可辨,留在她走过的

林间小道上,一直向前,通向

1405 黑暗的沼泽地,她拖走了

那位曾经与赫罗斯加一道

保家卫国的名臣的尸体。

英雄之子①行走在陡峭的山崖上,　　① 指赫罗斯加。

脚下的路崎岖狭窄,仅能

1410 容纳一人,先前从没有人来此攀登,

只有水中妖魔在此落脚营生。

国王率领几位机智的军士

走在队伍的前头侦察地形。

突然,他发现眼前一丛丛树木

1415 都倒向一边,悬垂在灰白的巉岩上;

多阴森的森林!下面一口深潭,

血水在那里沸腾。所有的丹麦人,

包括丹麦人的朋友,无数王公贵族

to suffer,     for thane many,

1420   grief for hero every,     when Æschere's

on the lake-cliff    head they found.

    Flood bloody welled,     folk at gazed,

with hot gore.    Horn at times sang

urgent war-song.    Troop all sat down.

1425   Saw then through water    snake-kinds many,

strange sea-dragons    waves exploring,

also on ness-slopes    monsters lying,

who in morning time    often carry out

a sorrowful attack    on sail-road,

1430   serpents and wild beasts.    They away plunged,

bitter and wrath-bulged;    bright-sound they heard,

war-horn wailing.    One a Geats' man

with shaft-bow    of life deprived,

of wave-struggle,    so that in its heart stood

1435   war-arrow hard;    it in water was

at swimming the slower,    when it death seized,

Fast it was in waves    with boar-spears

point-barbed    hard pursued,

fiercely attacked,    and on ness dragged up,

1440   wondrous wave-thrasher;    men stared at

gruesome guest.    Geared himself Beowulf

in hero-garb,    no way for lire mourned;

must war-byrnie    by hands woven,

一个个叫苦连天，心如刀绞，

1420 原来，就在水潭边的岩石上，
他们发现了伊斯切尔的头颅！
再朝水潭看去，但见激流中
翻腾着污血。战斗的号角
一声声吹响，全体战士就地坐下。

1425 他们看见许多形状如蛇的怪物
在水面上巡逻，堤岸上还躺着
各种水怪，他们与大海上
那些常常在清晨出来作祟，
制造悲剧的蛇妖海兽没有两样。

1430 听见嘹亮的声音，号角的歌唱，
他们怒气冲冲，纷纷跃入水中，
消失在堤岸上。但其中一个怪物
被一位高特武士用箭射中，
在水中挣扎着一命呜呼，因为

1435 那锐利的箭正中它的心脏，
临死前它已游得十分缓慢。
带钩的长矛即刻把它团团围住，
大家七手八脚把怪物拖上岸：
这是波涛中一头奇异的野兽，

1440 武士们争先恐后过来围观。
贝奥武甫披上他的盔甲，
他早已将生死置之度外。
这次他全身披挂，为的是

broad and skill-bright,    waves explore,

1445   it the bone-chest    cover could,

so that him battle-grip    heart not might,

angry-foe's fierce-grasp    life scathe;

but the white helm    head protected,

that which mere-depths    mingle should,

1450   seek water-surge    with gold adorned,

clasped in lordly-bands,    as it in far-days

wrought weapons' smith,    wonderfully formed,

beset with swine-forms    so that it then no

blade nor battle-swords    to bite were able.

1455    Was not that then least    of power-aids

that him in need lent    spokesman Hrothgar's;

was the hilt-sword's    Hrunting name;

it was unequalled    of ancient treasures;

edge was iron,    with deadly patterns streaked,

1460   hardened with battle-blood;    never it in fight betrayed

man any    who it in hands grasped,

he who dreadful journeys    venture dared,

to folk-place of foes;    not was it first time

that it courage deed    commit must.

1465   Indeed not bore in mind    son of Ecglaf

of strength mighty,    what he before spoke

wine-drunk,    when he the weapon lent

to better swordsman;    self not dared

潜入水中探险,那一身戎装

1445 懂得如何掩护主人的躯体,
使它免遭仇敌的伤害与摧残。
那顶闪光的头盔用来保护
他的脑袋,它镶满了金子。
盔檐华丽无比,古代的铁匠

1450 早就知道如何把头盔锻造,并用
野猪的图案把它装饰,从那以后,
任何宝剑和刀刃都无法
把它砍穿,如今它将进入深潭,
搅动湍流,在凶险的水中搜索敌人。

1455 赫罗斯加的传令官安佛斯,
这一次也给了他莫大的支持:
他把霍朗丁宝剑交给贝奥武甫,
这是一把举世无双的古剑,
具有纯钢的锋刃、致命的花纹,

1460 鲜红的热血把它淬硬。战场上
它不会辜负任何人,只要你
把它提在手里,从事冒险事业,
敢于跟仇敌对阵。它已不是首次
创建英雄的业绩。艾格拉夫之子

1465 以勇力著名,当他将这件兵器
交到一位更强大的战士手里,
他早已把先前因喝醉了酒
说出的胡言乱语抛诸脑后。

under waves' strife      life to risk,

1470   bravery perform;      there he glory forfeited,

courage-fame.      Not was for the other thus,

when he him for battle      equipped had.

# PART SEVEN
## Beowulf Attacks Grendel's Mother

Beowulf spoke,      son of Ecgtheow:

"Think now, glorious      son of Halfdane,

1475   wise chieftain,      now I am for fray eager,

gold-friend of man,      what we earlier said,

if I in cause      of yours should

life lose,      that you for me ever would be,

having passed on,      in father's place.

1480   Be you protector      to my young retainers,

hand-companions,      if me battle takes;

so too you the treasures,      which you me gave,

Hrothgar beloved,      to Hygelac send on.

May then in the gold perceive      Geats' lord,

但他自己没有胆量进入

1470　波涛冒险，他因此声名扫地。

另外一个人则与他大不一样，

他已披挂停当，正准备上战场。


# 七

## 贝奥武甫战妖母

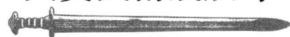

艾克塞奥之子贝奥武甫说：

"光荣的哈夫丹之子，智慧的国王，

1475　人民的朋友，我马上要投入战斗，

请你记住我们先前说过的话：

如果我为了援助你丢了性命，

一去不返，你将一如既往

把父亲应尽的责任承担：

1480　如果我不能活着回来，你就是

我的扈从和伙伴的保护人。

你给我的财宝，亲爱的赫罗斯加

请悉数转交给海格拉克。

高特人的国王，雷塞尔之子

1485   see, son of Hrethel,     when he on that treasure stares,

that I for generosity     a good king found,

rings' giver,     enjoyed while I was able.

And you Unferth let     old heirloom,

wondrous wave-sword     wide-known man

1490   hard-edged have;     I me with Hrunting

glory wreak,     or me death takes."

    After these words     Weder-Geats' prince

hurried bravely,     not at all answer

await would;     lake-surge enfolded

1495   battle-warrior.     Then was part of day

before he depth-land     discover might.

At once it saw,     she who floods' region

fiercely ravenous held     a hundred seasons,

grim and greedy,     that there of humans one

1500   monsters' land     from above explored.

Groped then towards,     warrior seized

in poison claws;     not the sooner inside she hurt

his hale body;     ring-mail outside protected,

so that she the war-dress     impale not might,

1505   linked limb-sark     with loathsome fingers.

    Bore then the lake-wolf,     when she to bottom came,

rings' chieftain     to court of hers,

so he not might,     however brave he was,

weapons wield,     but him monsters so many

1485　一旦看见这些金银财宝，
　　　就知道我遇上了慷慨的赐主，
　　　知道我曾经与他友好相处。
　　　我的传家宝，那把著名的宝剑
　　　就留给安佛斯，你手下的勇士。

1490　我将用他的名剑霍朗丁
　　　建立功勋，否则就让死神降临！"
　　　说完这些话，高特人的王子
　　　没等回话就即刻下水，
　　　汹涌的波涛已将英雄吞没。

1495　他在水中游了很长时间
　　　才看见潭底。那贪得无厌、
　　　既凶狠又残忍的女妖占领
　　　这片水域已有半个世纪；
　　　她马上发现有人来自水上，

1500　闯入她这魔鬼的居地探险。
　　　她摸索到武士身边，伸出魔爪
　　　把他紧紧抓住。但她无法伤害
　　　他强壮的躯体：因为他全身披挂，
　　　任凭她有令人生畏的利爪

1505　也撕不开那护身的盔甲。
　　　湖中之狼只好带着高贵的王子
　　　潜入潭底，进入她的巢穴；
　　　尽管他英勇无比，但他无法
　　　挥动他的武器，许多水怪

1510    assailed in deep,     sea-beasts sundry

with battle-tusks     war-sark tore,

harried him horrors.     Then the hero observed

that he in hostile hall     of some sort was,

where him no water     at all scathed,

1515    nor him because of roof-hall     reach not might

onrush of flood;     firelight he saw,

clearly blazing     brightly shining.

     Saw then the good man     depth-monster,

mere-woman mighty;     force-thrust gave

1520    to battle-blade,     hand swing not pulled,

so that her on head     ring-sword yelled

greedy war-song.     Then the guest found out

that the battle-brand     bite would not,

life scathe,     but the edge failed

1525    the noble at need;     endured already many

hand-encounters,     helm often sheared,

doomed man's war-dress;     then was first time

for precious treasure     that its glory failed.

     Again was resolute,     no way in courage slow,

1530    of glories mindful     kinsman of Hygelac.

Threw then wave-marked sword     with ornaments bound

angry warrior,     so that it on earth lay,

strong and steel-edged;     strength trusted,

hand-grip of might.     So shall man do,

1510 用各种各样的獠牙在深潭里
    向他攻击,撕咬着他的盔甲。
    英雄发现自己身处一座
    弥漫着敌意的大厅,那里没有水
    把他围困,因为大厅的顶部

1515 已将洪流隔开,使它无法造成
    对人的伤害。他还看见一处火光
    把整个大厅照得透亮。
    然后他看清了那深渊恶魔,
    强悍的女妖,于是举剑刺去,

1520 他的手用尽了平生的气力,
    钢刃劈在她头上,唱起了战歌,
    但这来访者很快发现,这一击
    根本无法伤害她的性命,
    那刀刃辜负了高贵的王子:

1525 这把宝剑可谓久经沙场,
    常常将盔甲砍穿,使敌人
    一命归天。这件珍贵的宝器
    第一次败坏了自己的名声。
    然而,这位海格拉克的外甥

1530 牢记自己的荣誉,他意志坚定,
    勇气未丧半分。只见他怒气冲冲
    把锋利的宝剑丢过一边,
    他信得过自己的气力,那双
    强劲的巨手。任何男子汉

1535    when he in battle     gain intends

long-lasting praise;    not for his life cares.

    Seized then by shoulder,    no way for feud mourned,

War-Geats' leader    Grendel's mother;

thrust then battle-hard man,    now he enraged was,

1540    deadly-foe,    so that she on floor fell.

She him back quickly    requital paid

with grim grip    and him against her clasped;

stumbled then, weary-minded    warrior strongest,

foot-fighter,    so that he in fall was.

1545    She bestrode then the hall-guest    and her dagger drew

broad and bright-edged;    would her bairn avenge,

only offspring.    Him on shoulder lay

breast-net braided;    it protected life,

to point and to edge    entry withstood.

1550    Had then perished    son of Ecgtheow

under yawning depth,    Geats' champion,

unless him battle-byrnie    help provided,

war-net hardened,    and holy God

controlled war-victory;    wise Lord,

1555    heavens' Ruler,    it aright decided

easily    when he again stood up.


    Saw then among armour    victory-blessed blade,

old-sword giantish    with edges sturdy,

1535　想建千秋武功，他就是榜样。
　　　他此刻毫不在乎自己的存亡。
　　　高特人的领袖没有畏缩不前，
　　　他抓住格兰道尔母亲的肩膀，
　　　怀着满腔仇恨用力一推，

1540　这死敌顿时跌倒在地上。
　　　但她很快还以颜色，用利爪
　　　把贝奥武甫死死掐住，
　　　英勇无比的战士终于无力支持，
　　　踉跄了一会儿，便倒了下去。

1545　她于是骑在来访者的身上，
　　　抽出明晃晃的刀要替儿子报仇。
　　　幸亏他身上那一副胸甲
　　　再次救了他的命，女妖的刀无论
　　　是砍是刺，都伤不着他的身。

1550　如果没有这副坚固的甲胄，
　　　艾克塞奥之子，高特人的冠军
　　　早就葬身于这豁裂的深渊——
　　　但神圣的上帝把握着胜负，
　　　英明的主，天上的统治者

1555　主持正义，决定让贝奥武甫
　　　轻松地从地上一跃而起。


　　　这时他发现挂着的甲胄背后
　　　有一把古代巨人锻造的神剑，

warriors' honour;　　it was weapon choicest,

1560　but it was bigger　　than any man other

　　　to battle-play　　bear was able,

　　　good and handsome,　　giants' handiwork.

　　　He seized then ring-hilt,　　champion of Scyldings

　　　bristling and battle-grim,　　ring-sword swung

1565　of life despairing,　　angrily struck,

　　　so that her on neck　　sharply it bit,

　　　bone-rings broke;　　blade all through-ran

　　　doomed flesh-cloak;　　she on floor sank,

　　　sword was bloody,　　man in work rejoiced.

1570　　Gleamed the glimmer,　　light within stood,

　　　even as from heaven　　brightly shines

　　　sky's candle.　　He around cavern looked;

　　　turned then by wall,　　weapon raised

　　　hard by hilts　　Hygelac's thane

1575　angry and resolute,　　was not the edge useless

　　　to battle-fighter,　　but he fast wished

　　　Grendel to repay　　war-onslaughts many

　　　which he had made　　against West-Danes

　　　more often much　　than on one attack,

1580　when he Hrothgar's　　hearth-companions

　　　slew in slumber,　　sleeping devoured

　　　of folk of Danes　　fifteen men,

　　　and other such　　out off-carried,

它是武士的光荣,兵器中的极品,
1560　比任何武士战场上使用的兵器
　　　都大了许多,巨人的杰作,
　　　既珍贵又美观。贝奥武甫
　　　提剑在手,为丹麦人而战的武士
　　　已经杀得正酣,只见他不顾一切
1565　挥舞着神剑,怀着满腔怒火,
　　　一剑击中女妖的脖颈,砍断
　　　她的肩骨。锋利的刀刃刺穿
　　　该死的躯体;女妖轰然倒下。
　　　宝剑鲜血淋淋,战士额手称庆。

1570　魔窟里火光冲天,白晃晃一片,
　　　就像那根天烛在空中照耀。
　　　贝奥武甫环顾洞府四周,
　　　把宝剑紧紧握在手里,沿着
　　　洞壁搜索。海格拉克的勇士
1575　怒气未消,随时准备继续战斗,
　　　他要与格兰道尔算清总账,
　　　因为他多次袭击丹麦人,
　　　每次少不了有十五位武士
　　　在梦睡中被他一一杀害,

1580　受害者都是赫罗斯加的亲信,
　　　这些丹麦人临死前睡得正香,
　　　他却把他们填进了饥肠。
　　　每次被他劫走的也有那么多,

hideous haul.    He him its reward paid,

1585    angry fighter,    in that he on bed saw

battle-weary    Grendel lying,

lifeless,    as him earlier injured

conflict at Heorot.    Corpse open burst,

when it after death    blow suffered,

1590    sword-stroke brutal,    and its then head he cut off.

Suddenly it saw    wise men

who with Hrothgar    at lake looked,

that was wave-swirl    all stirred up,

water with blood streaked.    Grey-maned,

1595    old, about the good man    together they spoke,

said that they the hero    again not thought

that he victory-exultant    to seek would come

the glorious ruler;    then many agreed

that him the sea-wolf    destroyed had.

1600    Then came ninth-hour of day.    Ness abandoned

intrepid Scyldings;    departed home thence

gold-friend of men.    Guests sat

at heart sick    and into mere stared;

wished and not expected    that they their friend-lord

1605    himself would see.    Then the sword began

from battle-blood    in deadly icicles

war-blade to wane;    it was a wonder great,

that it all melted    ice most-like,

那是何等可憎可恨的战利品!

1585 愤怒的战士要他还清这笔血债。

然而,他发现格兰道尔躺在地上

已经咽气,因为鹿厅那一仗

给了他致命的一击。恶魔已死,

硕大的尸体还得再挨一刀:

1590 贝奥武甫砍下了他的头颅。

岸上,智者们与赫罗斯加

一道望着水面,突然发现

水波涌起,潭水已被鲜血染红。

白发苍苍的将领们开始议论,

1595 都说他们的英雄已无指望,

他不可能再次胜利而归,

不可能从水中出来,再见

光荣的国王。他们一致相信

那海狼已残害了他的性命。

1600 时间已是下午三点。英勇的丹麦人

开始撤出山冈。武士的朋友

回到自己的王宫。但高特的武士

心情沮丧,仍守望着水面。

他们希望——明知希望渺茫——

1605 再见到他们敬爱的领袖。

这时,那把沾满鲜血的神剑

开始熔化,兵器变成了冰柱。

这真是一个不可思议的奇迹,

when frost's bond     Father loosens,

1610    unwinds water-ropes,     who control has

of times and seasons;     he is true Creator.

Not took he in those halls,     Weder-Geats' leader,

rich-possessions more,     though he there many saw,

than the head    and the hilt as well

1615    with gold adorned;     sword already melted,

burned up wave-streaked blade;     was the blood that hot,

poisonous alien,    who there inside perished.

At once was swimming     he who before in fight survived

battle-death of enemies,     water up through-dove;

1620    were wave-surges    all purged,

mighty regions,    when the alien

gave up life-days    and this loaned existence.

Came then to land    sea-men's leader

stout-hearted swimming;     in sea-loot rejoiced,

1625    mighty burden    which he him with had.

Went him then to meet,     God they thanked,

thrusting thane-band,     for chief they thrilled,

that they him safe    see might.

Then was from the agile hero     helm and byrnie

1630    quickly loosened.    Lake drowsed,

water under clouds,     with death-blood flecked.

Fared forth thence    by foot-tracks

in hearts happy,    earth-way paced,

神剑竟如融冰般化为乌有,

1610 就像天上掌管时令的父

化解冻结的霜雪。他是真正的造物主。

虽然高特人的领袖发现

洞府里有无数的金银财宝,但他

一概不取,只拿了魔怪的头颅

1615 和那把镶金的剑柄,那刀刃

已经熔化殆尽。魔怪的血太热,

那已死的精灵浑身是毒。

仇敌已死,而他仍然活着,

现在他飞快地在水中潜游;

1620 可怕的精灵一旦丧生,离开

这暂住的世界,那汹涌的浪涛,

广阔的水域,已经平静安澜。

水手的首领意志坚强,终于

游回岸上。他充满喜悦,

1625 随身带回沉甸甸的海底收获。

他的部属过来迎接他,向上帝

表示谢意,为能再次见到

他们的首领平安归来而欣喜。

大伙七手八脚帮勇士脱下

1630 头盔和胸甲。潭水已归平静,

天幕下只见一片鲜血点染的水面。

他们兴高采烈,踏上归途,

那羊肠小道已是他们的熟路。

known roads;     king-bold men

1635   from the lake-cliff    head carried

arduously    for them all

stout-hearted;    four had

on the spear-shafts    awkwardly to ferry

to the gold-hall    Grendel's head,

1640   until presently    to hall came

bold war-keen    fourteen

of the Geats marching;    man-lord with

proud in among    mead-plains trod.

Then came in walking    lord of thanes,

1645   deed-bold man    by glory honoured,

hero battle-brave,    Hrothgar to greet.

Then was by mane    on floor brought

Grendel's head,    where men were drinking,

awesome for earls    and the woman too,

1650   spectacle shocking;    men at stared.

国王手下的勇士抬着那头颅

1635　十分艰难地行进在山崖上，
　　　他们的意志个个无比坚强。
　　　格兰道尔的头颅被绑在
　　　长矛的杆子上，四个壮汉
　　　抬得上气不接下气，返回

1640　金碧辉煌的大厦。高特武士
　　　一行十四人徒步而行，最后
　　　全部回到鹿厅。他们的领袖
　　　走在他们中间，怀着无比
　　　自豪的心情。武士的首领，

1645　敢作敢为的男子汉，战场上的英雄
　　　带着无上荣耀参见赫罗斯加。
　　　格兰道尔的头颅被人抓住头发
　　　拖进那座用于宴乐的大厅。
　　　那丑陋的怪物真够吓人，

1650　在场的男女无不诧异万分。

# PART EIGHT
## Further Celebration at Heorot

Beowulf spoke,    son of Ecgtheow:

"Well, we you these sea-loots,    son of Halfdane,

lord of Scyldings,    gladly brought

glory's token,    which you here at look.

1655    I it not easily    with life survived,

war under water,    work risked

with difficulty;    at once was

battle ended    unless me God shielded.

Not could I in fight    with Hrunting

1660    anything achieve,    though the weapon is good;

but me granted    men's Ruler

that I on wall saw    handsome hanging

old-sword supreme    —most often He has guided

friendless man—    so that I the weapon drew.

1665    I killed then in the fight,    when me chance allowed,

house's guardians.    Then the battle-blade

burned up, wave-streaked sword,    as the blood sprang out,

hottest battle-sweat.    I the hilt thence

from foes brought back;    foul-deeds avenged,

1670    slaughter of Danes,    as it fitting was.

# 八
# 鹿厅再祝捷

艾格塞奥之子贝奥武甫说：
"哈夫丹之子，希尔德人的国王，
我们很高兴为你带来这些战利品，
其为光荣的见证，这你已亲眼看见。
1655 这次我能活着回来并非易事，
那场水战，我所履行的任务
充满风险；如果没有上帝庇护，
那场战斗即刻就会宣告结束。
尽管霍朗丁是一把名剑，
1660 但战斗中却发挥不了作用。
亏得人类的统治者——他常常
为无依无靠的人指点迷津——
让我见到一把古代的巨剑
挂在墙上，正好供我使唤。
1665 我于是瞄准时机，乱战中
杀死洞府中的妖魔。当滚烫的鲜血
喷涌而出，饰有波纹的宝剑
即刻熔化。我从仇敌那里
只带回一截剑柄。我义不容辞
1670 向屠杀丹麦人的恶魔报仇雪耻。

I it you then promise,      that you in Heorot may

sorrowless sleep      with your soldiers' company,

and thanes all      of your nation,

veterans and youth,      that you for them dread not need,

1675    chieftain of Scyldings,      on that score,

life-evil for heroes,      as you did before."

      Then was golden hilt      to ageing man,

to hoary battle-leader      in hand given,

giants' ancient work;      it to possession passed,

1680    after devils' fall,      of Danes' lord,

wonder-smiths' work;      and then this world gave up

grim-hearted creature,      God's enemy,

of murder guilty,      and his mother too;

into keeping passed      of world-kings

1685    the finest      between seas

of those who in Danish lands      treasures' dealt out.

      Hrothgar spoke,      hilt examined,

old heirloom,      on it was origin inscribed

of former strife,      when flood slew,

1690    ocean gushing,      giants' kin,

fatally they fared;      that was alien tribe

to eternal Lord;      them the end-reward

through waters' rush      Ruler granted.

Also was on the hilt-shanks      of shining gold

1695    in rune-staves      rightly marked,

我向你保证,从今后你和你的将士

尽可以高枕无忧睡在宴乐厅,

丹麦人的国王,你再不必

为你的老少臣民担惊受怕,因为

1675　死亡再不会像先前那样

无端降临在你的百姓身上。"

那金色的剑柄,古代巨人的杰作

呈献在老人面前,交到

白发苍苍的武士手中。恶魔一死,

1680　铁匠制造的神器成了

丹麦王的财产。歹毒的怪物,

上帝的死敌,由于恶贯满盈,

终于与他母亲一起弃绝人寰,

宝物最后落到赫罗斯加手里,

1685　他是四海之内最贤明的国王,

北方部落中财产的赐主。

赫罗斯加仔细端详剑柄,

占老的传家宝,那上面铭刻着

早期争战的事迹,那时洪水泛滥,

1690　滔滔的大水席卷了巨人族;

他们是永恒的上帝的异端,

万能的统治者用滔滔洪水

对他们做出末日的判决。

在宝剑金光闪闪的护手上,

1695　还有几行北欧古文,记载着

set down and said,    for whom the sword made,

of irons most excellent,    first had been,

writhe-hilted and serpent-marked.    Then the wise spoke

son of Halfdane;    fell silent all:

1700       "That indeed may say,    he who truth and right

performs among folk,    far-back all recalls,

old homeland-guard,    that this hero was

born better.    Glory is raised up

through wide-ways,    friend my Beowulf,

1705    your over nations each.    All you it patiently control,

strength with heart's wisdom.    I to you shall my fulfil

friendship, as we earlier said.    You shall as comfort be

all long-lasting    to nation your,

to heroes a help.    Not was Heremod so

1710    to sons of Ecgwela,    to Honour-Scyldings;

not grew he for their pleasure,    but for slaughter

and for death-killing    of Danish people;

felled in fury-mood    feast-companions,

close comrades,    until he alone passed,

1715    famous chieftain    man's joys from,

although him mighty God    with strength's delights

powerfully supported,    above all men

forth furthered.    Yet to him in heart grew

breast-thoughts blood-thirsty;    not at all rings gave

1720    to Danes for glory;    joyless survived,

这纯钢的宝剑最初为谁铸造；

剑柄上还弯弯曲曲铭刻有

蛇的图案。智慧的哈夫丹之子

这时开口说话,大厅一片寂静:

1700 "作为一位部落的保卫者,

一个为百姓捍卫真理和正义的人,

那遥远的往事我记得一清二楚:

但这样的英雄却从未听说。

贝奥武甫,我的朋友,你的英名

1705 将四海颂扬,妇孺皆知。你的智慧

牢牢地掌握着你的神力。

我会信守诺言,与你保持友谊。

你将永远是人民的安慰,

武士的后盾。但那海勒摩德

1710 对待艾克瓦拉①的子孙,光荣的丹麦人       ① 早期丹麦的
                                              国王。
就不是如此。他建功立业,带给人民

不是幸福,而是屠杀与痛苦。

他气势汹汹,杀死宴乐的伙伴,

亲密的战友,直到这臭名昭著的国王

1715 变成孤家寡人,享受不到人间温暖,

尽管全能的上帝曾经使他

权势显赫,踌躇满志,凌驾于

万民之上。然而,他骨子里

已变得嗜血成性:对于丹麦人

1720 他从不赐予财宝。他活得凄凉,

so that he the struggle's    violence suffered,

affliction lengthy.    You learn by this,

manly virtue understand.    I this tale for you

told, in winters wise.    Wonder is to tell

1725  how mighty God    to mankind

through broad spirit    wisdom shares out,

land and noble qualities;    He has of all control.

At times He in delight    lets wander

man's inner thought    of glorious kin,

1730  gives him in homeland    earth's joy

to command,    stronghold of men,

renders to him as subject    world's regions,

broad kingdom,    so that he himself not may

in his unwisdom    end conceive.

1735  Dwells he in abundance,    not him at all hinders

sickness nor age,    nor him evil sorrow

in mind darkens,    nor strife anywhere

sword-violence shows,    but to him all world

wends at will;    he it worse not knows,


1740  until to him within    pride's portion

grows and prospers;    then the warder sleeps,

soul's guardian;    is the sleep too sound,

with cares encased,    killer very near,

he who from shaft-bow    foully shoots.

备受痛苦的煎熬,只因他争斗不息,

给人们带来无穷无尽的灾难。

你应引以为戒,慷慨为怀。

我年事已高,向你说说这段历史。

1725　万能的上帝胸怀博大,赋予

人类以智慧、土地和光荣,

这真是奇迹;主统辖一切。

主常常让出身高贵的人

扬扬自得,享受人间的荣华富贵,

1730　让他治理他的王国,百姓的堡垒,

让四方部落,那大大小小的王国

逐一在他面前俯首称臣,

于是,他便忘乎所以,再不想想

自己会有寿终正寝的一天。

1735　他堆金积玉,疾病与衰老

一概与他无涉,可怕的忧愁

从不笼罩他的心头,更没有敌人

向他寻衅报复,因为整个世界

都按他的意志运转;他无忧无虑——

1740　直到骄气在他身上滋生,

并日益膨胀;于是,灵魂的卫士

呼呼大睡,这一觉睡得太沉,

以致一切戒备消除,刽子手来到跟前,

向他射出置人于死地的毒箭。

1745    Then is in heart        under armour struck

with bitter arrow,        himself protect not can,

with twisted temptations        of terrible demon;

seems to him too little        what he long held,

covets cruel-minded,        never proudly gives

1750    golden rings,        and he then whole world

forgets and forsakes,        that which him before God gave,

glory's Ruler,        honour's share.

It in ending        finally happens,

that the body        loaned declines,

1755    fated, it falls;        another inherits,

who heedlessly        treasures deals out,

hero's ancient wealth,        horror not heeds.

        Guard you from this base evil,        Beowulf beloved,

hero supreme,        and for you the better choose,

1760    eternal gains;        arrogance shun,

famed champion!        Now is your strength's glory

for a while;        in turn soon will be

that you sickness or sword-edge        of strength will strip,

or fire's embrace,        or flood's surge,

1765    or bite of blade,        or spear's flight,

or horrid old-age;        or eyes' brightness

dims and darkens;        suddenly will be,

that you, warrior,        death overpowers.

        So I Ring-Danes        hundred seasons

1745　锐利的箭镞带着恶魔的号令

　　　　穿过他的盔甲,射中他的心脏;

　　　　而他却无法保护自己,于是,

　　　　他开始不满足于已占有的一切,

　　　　变得贪得无厌,舍不得分赐

1750　镀金的项圈,他已经忘记

　　　　自己的一切均来自上帝,否认

　　　　是天上的主宰赐予他人间的光荣。

　　　　到头来那具借来的躯壳

　　　　逐渐虚弱,不可避免地走向死亡;

1755　那时将有另外一人把财产继承,

　　　　而他对钱财却随意挥霍,

　　　　丝毫不知道对它们严加看管。

　　　　亲爱的贝奥武甫,超凡的英雄,

　　　　你千万不要养成这样的恶习,

1760　你应该学好样,万古流芳,

　　　　戒除骄气,做一名伟大的武士!

　　　　武力的荣耀犹如过眼云烟,

　　　　疾病和争战很快会把你的力量耗尽,

　　　　摧残人生的还有烈火的毒舌,

1765　洪水的波涛,刀剑的撞击,

　　　　长矛的飞舞,可怕的衰老;

　　　　武士啊,明亮的双眸总要失明,

　　　　那时死神就来到了你身边。

　　　　我在苍天下统治富有的丹麦人

1770 ruled under sky,      and them in war defended

from many tribes     upon this middle-earth

with spears and swords,    so that I for me any

under heaven's expanse    enemy not counted.

Well, me for that in homeland    setback came,

1775 grief after gladness,    since Grendel became,

ancient fighter,    invader my;

I from that attack    endlessly endured

mind-care massive.    For that be to Maker thanks,

to eternal Lord,    that I alive survived

1780 so that I on the head    sword-bloodied

after ancient strife    with eyes might stare.

    Go now to bench,    banquet-pleasure take,

war-honoured:    we shall very many

treasures share    when morning comes."

1785     Geat was glad-hearted,    went at once away,

bench to seek,    as the wise king ordered.

Then was again as before    for bold warriors,

for hall-sitters,    fine feast prepared

a second time.    Night-helm grew dim,

1790 dark over retinue.    Company all arose,

wished grey-maned king    bed to seek,

aged Scylding.    Geat strongly indeed,

famed shield-fighter,    to rest desired;

at once him hall-thane    man of journey weary,

1770 已有几十个年头,我用长矛和宝剑
     保卫他们不受众多部落的侵犯,
     我原以为在这广袤的天地间
     从此再不会有仇敌出现。
     哎呀,真是乐极生悲,当那宿敌

1775 格兰道尔侵犯我的家园,
     不幸即刻在我身上降临。
     长期以来,我因他的骚扰
     而惶惶不安。感谢造物主,
     永恒的上帝,我能在有生之年

1780 亲眼看见那场酷烈的争斗
     以及恶魔那颗血淋淋的头颅。
     请英雄入座,你已扬名在战场,
     现在就开怀畅饮吧。明天一早,
     我还要赏你无数金银财宝。"

1785 高特人听后好不喜欢,即刻
     遵照国王的吩咐找到自己的座位。
     丰盛的宴席再次摆设停当,
     与上次一样,众勇士济济一堂
     欢庆胜利,直到夜幕降临,

1790 夜色盖过勇士们的身影。
     全体起立,白发苍苍的国王
     打算回宫就寝。勇武的高特人
     此时也正需要解甲休息。
     于是,即刻有一位大厅侍者

1795     from far country,      forth guided,

who for courtesy      all attended

thane's needs,      such as in those days

warrior-sailors      to have were bound

    Rested him then open-hearted;      hall towered,

1800     gabled and gold-adorned;      guest within slept,

until raven black      heaven's joy

glad-hearted greeted.      Then came bright hurrying

shine against shadow,      warriors hastened,

were noble ones      back to people

1805     eager to fare;      wished far thence

guest brave-spirited      ship to seek.

    Told then the tough man      Hrunting to wear,

son of Ecglaf,      told his sword to take,

beloved iron,      said him for loan thanks,

1810     said he the war-friend      worthy counted,

fight-powerful,      not in words insulted

sword's edge;      he was proud man.

And then journey-eager,      in armour ready

warriors were;      went man dear to Danes

1815     noble to high seat,      where the other was;

hero battle-bold      Hrothgar greeted.

1795　来为疲惫的远方来客领路；

　　　　他彬彬有礼为勇士们效劳，

　　　　关怀备至就像对待远航的水手，

　　　　让他们获得最满意的享受。

　　　　这灵魂高尚的人终于安寝，

1800　鹿厅高高矗立，金碧辉煌，

　　　　客人进入梦乡，直到渡鸦欢噪，

　　　　宣告天已破晓。明亮的晨光

　　　　忙于把阴影驱赶。勇士们

　　　　急急起床，迫切登上归程，回到

1805　亲友们中间。勇敢的来宾

　　　　打算乘船返回自己的家园。

　　　　无畏的勇士让人拿过霍朗丁宝剑，

　　　　他把这件珍贵的兵器交还给

　　　　艾格拉夫之子。他向他表示谢意，

1810　称这剑为战士之友，锋利无比，

　　　　在他的言辞中，丝毫没有

　　　　贬低之意。他是个出言谨慎的人。

　　　　这时，勇士们都已披挂停当，

　　　　急于上路。深受丹麦人喜爱的王子

1815　来到另外一位王者的宝座前：

　　　　善战的贝奥武甫向赫罗斯加致意。

# PART NINE
## Beowulf Returns Home

Beowulf spoke,     son of Ecgtheow:
"Now we sea-farers     say will,
from far off come,     that we are eager
1820   Hygelac to seek.     Were here worthily
at will entertained;     you us well treated.
If I then on earth     anything may
of your heart's love     more earn,
warriors' lord,     than I yet did,
1825   with war-deeds,     I am ready at once.
If I it find out     over flood's expanse
that you neighbour-tribes     with terror threaten,
as you enemies     sometimes did,
I you thousand     thanes will bring,
1830   heroes as help.     I of Hygelac know,
Geats' lord,     although he young is,
folk's guardian,     that he me support will
with words and actions,     so that I you well honour
and you as aid     spear-shafts bear,
1835   force's strength,     where you are men-needy.
If him then Hrethric     to courts of Geats

# 九
## 贝奥武甫回国

艾克塞奥之子贝奥武甫说：
"我们这班来自远方的水手
现在有言奉告：我们急欲返回
1820　海格拉克身边。我们在贵国
称心如意，受到盛情款待。
战士的恩主，假如在这世上
还有别的机会让我一展身手，
就像先前我建立战功那样，
1825　我会随时听从您的召唤。
在大洋彼岸，只要我有所耳闻，
知道有某个邻国以武力相威胁，
一如您过去的仇敌那样前来侵犯，
我定会率领上千名精兵
1830　为您排忧解难。我了解海格拉克，
高特人的国王，他作为人民的护主
虽然年轻，但一定会以实际言行
诚心诚意支持我，只要您需要，
我一定能为您搬来救兵，
1835　用手中的长矛为您增援效劳。
还有，如果赫里斯雷克王子

decides to go, ruler's son,    he may there many

friends find;    far countries are

better sought    by one who himself is strong."

1840    Hrothgar spoke    to him in answer:

"You these word-sayings    wise Lord

in mind sent;    not heard I more intelligent

at so young age    man make speech.

You are of power strong    and in heart knowing,

1845    wise word-speaker.    Likely I reckon,

if it comes about    that from you spear takes,

battle sword-fierce,    Hrethel's heir,

disease or iron    ruler your,

folk's guardian,    and you your life have,

1850    that the Sea-Geats    better not have

to choose    king any other,

hoard-guard of heroes,    if you rule will

kinsmen's kingdom.    Me your mind-heart

pleases for long thus well,    dear Beowulf.

1855    Have you achieved    that for folk shall,

for Geats' people    and for Spear-Danes,

peace be mutual    and strife subside,

hostilities    which they in past endured,

shall be, while I wield    wide kingdom,

1860    treasures shared;    many a man another

with good gifts will greet    over gannet's bath;

乐意光临高特人的宫廷，

他一定能交上许多朋友；

伟大的远方客人永远受欢迎。"

1840　国王赫罗斯加这样回答他：

"全能的主赋予你这般好口才，

你年纪轻轻，说话却如此得体，

这我以前从未听说。你不仅

勇力过人，智慧超群，而且

1845　善于辞令。如果雷塞尔之子，

你们的国王，人民的统治者，

在战场上遇到什么不测，

或者疾病和利刃夺走他的生命，

而你那时仍健康地活在人间，

1850　我想，高特人当中再挑不出

比你更合适的人选做国王，

财富的保护者，只要你自己

乐意治理国家。亲爱的贝奥武甫，

你的品行真让我无比欢喜。

1855　你给所有的高特人和丹麦人

带来了和平；争斗与敌意，

先前那么猖獗，都将因你而消弭。

只要我一直治理这个国家，

我会让大家分享我们的财富，

1860　不管是谁来自大洋彼岸，

我都要让他得到丰厚的奖赏。

shall ring-prow      over ocean bring

gifts and love-tokens,      I that nation know

both to foe and to friend      firmly disposed,

1865　entirely faultless      in the ancient fashion."

　　　Again to him earls' protector      in hall gave,

son of Halfdane,      treasures twelve;

told him with these gifts      nation dear

to seek in safety,      quickly return.

1870　Kissed then      king the noble good,

chieftain of Scyldings      thane best

and by neck embraced;      fell from him tears,

from grey-haired king.      In him were two thoughts,

old and deeply wise,      one stronger,

1875　that they again never      meet would,

brave in council.      Was to him the man so dear,

that he the breast-surge      hold back not might;

but him in heart      in thought-bonds fixed

for dear man      hidden longing

1880　burned in blood.      Him Beowulf thence,

war-man gold-proud      grass-mould trod,

in treasure triumphing;      sea-walker awaited

owner-lord,      as it at anchor rode.

Then was on journey      gift of Hrothgar

1885　often praised;      that was one king

entirely blameless,      until him age deprived

金碧辉煌的帆船将满载礼物和友谊

漂过茫茫大海。我了解贵国人民，

他们的品德无可挑剔，让我们

1865　齐心协力，永结友好，同仇敌忾。"

说完，哈夫丹之子，王公的保护人

在宴乐厅又赏赐了贝奥武甫十二件宝贝，

并嘱咐他带着这份厚礼

平安返回家乡，尽快再访丹麦。

1870　高贵的国王，丹麦人的首领，

亲吻了最杰出的战士，并与他

热烈拥抱。白发苍苍的恩主

早已热泪盈眶。这年迈的智者

怀着两种思想，其中一种更其强烈——

1875　他心里明白，经此一别，两位勇士

从此再无重逢的希望。他对贝奥武甫

实在太感亲切，禁不住心潮澎湃，

因为在他的内心，对这位可爱的人

怀着深深的爱惜，此番情意燃烧在

1880　他的血液里。贝奥武甫终于告辞，

光荣的战士带着金银财宝

喜气洋洋踏上绿草地。航船抛着锚，

正等待它的主人的到来。

一路上，战士们交口夸奖

1885　赫罗斯加的礼物。作为国王

他无可挑剔，但岁月无情，

of strength's delights,     which often many has harmed.

       Came then to flood     full-hearted

       young-warriors' band;     ring-mail they wore,

1890   linked limb-sarks.     Land-guard observed

       return of heroes    as he before did;

       not he with scorn    from cliff's height

       guests greeted,    but them to meet rode,

       said that welcome    Wederas' people

1895   fighters bright-armoured    to ship fared.

       Then was on sand    sea-curved boat

       laden with war-clothes,    ringed-prow

       with horses and treasures;    mast towered

       over Hrothgar's    hoard-wealth.

1900    He the boat-guard    bound-gold

       sword gave    so that he after was

       on mead-bench    by treasure the worthier,

       by heirloom.    Put out ship

       to disturb deep water,    Danes' land left.

1905   Then was by mast    a sea-sheet mighty,

       sail by rope fastened;    sea-beam boomed;

       not there wave-floater    wind over billows

       journey hindered;    sea-walker fared,

       floated foamy-necked    forth over swell,

1910   bound prow    over ocean streams,

最终将耗尽他生命的力量。


勇敢而年轻的一群战士
来到海岸边。他们一个个披甲戴盔，
1890　全副武装。守卫海岸的哨长
又见到这一队凯旋的英雄。
这一次他不再厉声吆喝，而是
策马下了山冈迎接，他还说
勇士们全身披挂乘船返回家园，
1895　一定会受到高特人热烈欢迎。
这时，那只泊在沙滩上的木舟
装载了盔甲、马匹和金银财宝，
赫罗斯加所赠送的诸多礼物
就堆在高耸入云的桅杆下。
1900　贝奥武甫然后送给航船的看护者①　　①　指哨长。
一把镶金的宝剑，使他从今往后
在宴会上能凭此宝物大出风头。
航船终于推出沙滩，进入深水，
驶离丹麦人居住的土地。
1905　武士们用绳子张起一面巨帆，
桅杆发出吱吱嘎嘎的声响。
海风无法阻止这海上的漂浮器
行进在浪涛上；帆船起航，
船首划破水面，激起层层浪花，
1910　行进在汹涌的波涛上，直到

163

until they Geats' cliffs     make out might,

well-known nesses;     keel up surged

wind-driven,     on land stood.

     Quick was at water     harbour-guard waiting,

1915     he who already long time     for loved men

eager at current     far gazed.

Roped into sand     broad-bosomed ship

by anchor-bonds firm,     lest waves' force

timbers handsome     break up might.

1920     Ordered then ashore to bear     heroes' treasure

jewels and plated gold;     was not for them far thence

to seek     wealth's wielder,

Hygelac Hrethel's son,     where at home dwelt

self with retainers     to sea-wall near.

1925     Building was beautiful,     bold-famed king,

high in hall,     Hygd very young,

wise, well-thriving,     though winters few

in stronghold     lived had

Hæreth's daughter;     not was she mean, however,

1930     nor too grudging of gifts     to Geats' people,

of treasure-wealth.     Modthryth committed,

fine folk-queen,     fearful crimes;

not one dared     bold to risk

of dear retainers,     except great lord,

1935     that at her by day     with eyes he looked;

高特的悬崖,那熟悉的海岬
依稀可见。木舟借着风力
快速进港,终于停靠在岸边。
海港卫士即刻来到沙滩上,

1915　他一直眺望大海,急切等待
他所尊敬的战士返回家乡。
贝奥武甫把船靠上岸,并用缆绳
紧紧拴住,唯恐汹涌的潮水
把这漂亮的木舟远远冲走。

1920　然后他吩咐战士把金银财宝
悉数搬上岸。不久,他们见到
财富的赐予者,国王海格拉克,
雷塞尔的儿子:他与他的臣属
就居住在离海岸不远的宫廷里。

1925　王宫金碧辉煌,勇敢的国王
高高在上,年轻的王后希格德
不仅聪慧过人,而且举止高雅,
尽管这位海勒斯的公主在王宫
才居住了几个春秋。她慷慨大方,

1930　从来不吝啬向高特人奖赏财物。
而那莫德莱丝王后就不是这样,
她年轻时做过许多可怕的坏事,
除了她的父王,任何臣属
都不敢在大白天抬起眼睛

1935　看一看她的容颜。除非

but for him deadly bonds  waited he reckoned,

hand-plaited;  quickly then was

after seizure  sword appointed,

that it patterned blade  settle would,

1940 death-woe declare.  Not is such queenly custom

for woman to practise,  though she unique be,

that peace-weaver  of-life deprives

on lying-charge  loved man.

  However, it remedied  Hemming's kinsman;

1945 ale-drinkers  otherwise said,

that she people-harm  less practised,

malice-spites,  since first she was

given gold-adorned  to young warrior

of lineage noble,  when she Offa's hall

1950 over fallow flood  by father's counsel

in voyage sought;  there she later well

on throne,  for goodness famed,

life's destiny  living enjoyed,

held high love  for heroes' lord,

1955 of all mankind,  by my knowledge,

the finest  between seas

of mighty race;  because Offa was

in gifts and battles,  spear-brave man,

widely honoured,  in wisdom ruled

1960 homeland his;  to him Eomer was born

他想领教被人捆绑的滋味。

一旦被逮住,锋利的刀刃

就将架上他的脖颈,宣告

死亡的悲痛已在他的眼前。

1940 身为王家的闺秀如此行事

实在不妥,尽管她的美无与伦比,

但编织和平的女子①不应该

因虚构的伤害处死可爱的人。

亏得海敏的后人②结束了这场灾难。

1945 宴席上说故事的人还说,

她后来听从了父亲的教诲,

披金戴银嫁给了年轻的武士,

那受人尊敬的贵族。她渡过

茫茫大海,来到奥法的宫廷,

1950 从此以后,她不再伤害无辜,

作弄他人。在王后的宝座上,

她后来还以慷慨闻名于世,

在她的有生之年,她深深爱着

那位武士的首领。据我所知,

1955 她的夫君是人间的大伟人,

普天之下,四海之内,谁也不能

与他相提并论。由于奥法

文武双全,所以深受子民的爱戴,

他以智慧治理自己的国家。

1960 后来奥法生下儿子奥玛尔,

① 为了缓和部落间的矛盾,一国的公主常常嫁到敌国,故有"编织和平的女子"一说。
② 指下文传说中的麦西亚国王奥法,此人可能是与之同名的麦西亚国王奥法二世(757—796)的祖先。

167

for heroes as help,     Hemming's kinsman,

grandson of Garmund,     in battle strong.


    Walked then the hardy hero     with his hand-picked men

self along sand,     sea-plain treading,

1965   wide foreshores.     World-candle shone,

sun from south eager.     They journey ended,

swiftly strode     to where heroes' shield,

slayer of Ongentheow,     stronghold within,

young battle-king     good they heard

1970   rings doled out.     To Hygelac was

coming of Beowulf     quickly reported,

that there in homestead     warriors' defender,

shield-companion     living came,

from battle-play unharmed     to court walking.

1975   Quickly was cleared,     as the mighty king bade,

for foot-guests     floor within.

    Sat then with him     he who the fight survived,

kinsman to kinsman,     after liege-lord

in formal speech     loyal thane greeted,

1980   in sincere words.     With mead-cups passed

through the hall-room     Hæreth's daughter,

loved the people,     goblets bore

to heroes' hands.     Hygelac began

his retainer     in hall the high

这海敏的后代,加蒙德的孙子
作战勇敢,不愧为武士的脊梁。


再说勇敢的贝奥武甫,他率领
亲手挑选的战士沿着沙滩
1965　行走在海岸上。高照的天烛,
从南方匆匆而来。旅程结束了,
此刻他们正急急走向城堡,
他们听说那王公的保护人,
奥根索的夺命者①,他们的好国王
1970　正在那里分赏金银财宝。
贝奥武甫归来的消息很快通报国王,
海格拉克得知武士的保护人,
他的战友,经过浴血争战,
已平安返回高特的宫廷。

1975　国王于是下令,即刻在大厅
为徒步的壮士腾出座位。
贝奥武甫用庄重而恭敬的言辞
向他的主公表示敬意,然后
这位恶战的幸存者落座在
1980　国王身边,舅甥俩肩并着肩。
海勒斯的女儿手端酒杯穿过
大厅,热情地招呼众多宾客,
并把盛有美酒的杯子一一端到
勇士们面前。海格拉克怀着好奇心

① 奥根索是瑞
典人的国王,死
于海格拉克讨伐
瑞典的战争中,
但并非为高特国
王亲手所杀。

169

1985 fully to question,    him curiosity urged,

what Sea-Geats'    adventures were:

    "How fared you on journey,    dear Beowulf,

when you suddenly    far decided

battle to seek    over salt water,

1990 combat in Heorot?    Did you Hrothgar's

wide-known woe    at all amend,

for famed chieftain?    I with its anxiety

in sorrow-floods seethed,    venture not trusted

of beloved man;    I you long begged

1995 that you the slaughter-spirit    not at all confronted,

let South-Danes    selves settle

war with Grendel.    To God I thanks say,

that I you sound    see might."

    Beowulf spoke,    son of Ecgtheow:

2000     "It is no secret,    lord Hygelac,

the great meeting,    to many men,

what struggle-time    for me and Grendel

happened in that place,    where he all too many

for Victory-Scyldings    sorrows caused,

2005 misery for ever;    I it all avenged,

so boast not need    Grendel's kinsmen

any upon earth    of dawn-clash that,

he who longest lives    of loathed race,

in malice enmeshed.    I there first came

1985  彬彬有礼地询问他的外甥，
      想知道高特人此行经历的风险。
      "亲爱的贝奥武甫，当初你贸然决定
      渡过咸水的海洋，前往鹿厅
      寻求战斗，此次历险结果如何？

1990  你是否为赫罗斯加，那著名的国王
      解除了那世人皆知的祸患？
      我一直为你担忧，挂肚牵肠——
      因为我对亲人的冒险始终
      放心不下。我早就劝说过你，

1995  不要去惹那个吃人的妖魔，
      让丹麦人自己去跟格兰道尔周旋。
      看见你平安无事返回家乡，
      为此我要衷心感谢上苍。"
      艾克塞奥的儿子贝奥武甫说：

2000  "海格拉克国王，我们那场大战
      许多人已有耳闻，交战的双方
      是我和格兰道尔，地点就在
      那魔怪无数次给丹麦人
      制造许多痛苦和悲伤的地方。

2005  我已经为他们报仇雪恨，
      那些留在世上的格兰道尔同类
      无论活得多久，仇恨多深，
      从今往后都不能再吹嘘
      那天晚上的战斗。我首先进入

2010    to the ring-hall      Hrothgar to greet;

            at once to me the famed     son of Halfdane,

            when he heart-thought    mine knew,

            with his own sons     seat assigned.

            Company was content,     not saw I all my life

2015    under heaven's hollow     hall-sitters'

            mead-joy more.     At times famous queen,

            peace-pledge of peoples,    hall whole passed through,

            emboldened boys young;    often she twisted-ring

            to warrior gave,     before she to seat went.

2020     At times before retinue     daughter of Hrothgar

            to earls unending    ale-flagon bore,

            those I Frearwaru    hall-sitters

            call by name heard,    where she studded cup

            to heroes handed.    She promised is,

2025    young, gold-adorned,     to Ingeld, glad son of Froda;

            has this arranged    friend of Scyldings,

            kingdom's keeper,    and it wise counsel reckons

            that he with this woman    blood-feuds many,

            conflicts will settle.    Very seldom anywhere

2030    after leader's fall    for little while

            deadly spear lies idle,    though the bride is good.

            May this then displease    chief of Heatho-Bards

            and thanes all    of that tribe,

            when he with the woman    on hall-floor walks,

2010　　那座雄伟的大厅拜见赫罗斯加；
　　　　一俟著名的哈夫丹之子弄清
　　　　我的来意,他即刻腾出座位
　　　　让我与他的王子坐在一起。
　　　　大厅里喜气洋洋;普天之下,

2015　　我从未见过如此欢乐的场面。
　　　　那位著名的王后,和平的使者,
　　　　不时地穿梭在宴乐大厅,
　　　　向年轻人劝酒。归座以前,
　　　　她还多次向来宾分赐项圈。

2020　　赫罗斯加的公主也手持酒壶,
　　　　一次次来到王公贵族面前;
　　　　当她向众英雄端上镶金酒盅,
　　　　我听见大家都叫她弗莱瓦鲁。
　　　　她年纪轻轻,浑身珠光宝气,

2025　　她已经许配英格德,弗罗达①的儿子。

① 希索巴人的
国王。

　　　　这桩婚姻似乎有益于丹麦王,
　　　　王国的保护人,因为他相信,
　　　　通过这位公主,血仇和争端②

② 指丹麦人与
希索巴人之间的
血仇和争端。

　　　　就能从此了结。然而,任何一个王国,

2030　　只要某个王子倒下,致命的长矛
　　　　便不会入库,尽管那新娘非常善良。
　　　　将来某天,当他领着这位女子
　　　　进入宴乐厅,而丹麦人的子孙,
　　　　她的扈从,身上闪耀着祖传的宝物——

2035     that noble sons of Danes,     her retainers, are feasted;

on them glisten     ancient heirlooms,

hard and ring-adorned,     Heatho-Bards' treasure,

while they those weapons     to wield were able,

until they destroyed     in the shield-play

2040     dear companions     and their own lives.


      Then speaks out at beer-feast     he who ring sees,

aged spear-warrior,     he who all remembers,

spear-death of soldiers     —in him is fierce heart—

begins sad-minded     some young warrior's

2045     through heart's thought,     courage to test,

war-ruin to waken,     and these words speaks:

     'Can you, my friend, that sword recognise,

which your father     into fight bore

under war-mask     on last campaign,

2050     precious iron,     where him Danes slew,

ruled slaughter-field,     when Withergyld lay dead,

after heroes' fall,     fierce Scyldings?

Now here of those slayers     son of some one,

in finery exultant     on hall-floor walks,

2055     of murder boasts,     and the treasure wears,

which you by right     possess should.'

     He urges thus and reminds     again and again

with bitter words     until time comes

2035 我是说他们身佩从希索巴人那里
缴获的宝剑进入宴席，这时候，
希索巴国王和他的全体武士
都会不高兴，他们随时会挥舞
手中的武器，导致一场厮杀，
2040 使亲密的伙伴和他们自己死于非命。

宴席中会有一位希索巴老战士
当场认出这样一件传家宝，
唤起他对血腥屠杀的回忆，
他的心因悲伤而变得阴险，
2045 他于是开始试探某位年轻战士，
用这样的话激励他去拼杀：
'我的朋友，你认得那把宝剑吗？
你父亲曾佩带它参加最后一次战斗，
但那丹麦人，凶恶的希尔德子孙
2050 杀害了他，占领了争战的地方，
武士们一个个倒在战场上，
威塞哥尔德也剑下身亡。
但如今凶手的儿子却趾高气扬
在大厅里走来走去，吹嘘
2055 那场屠杀。他身上佩带的宝剑
本来应该挂在你的身上。'
他不失时机用这样刻薄的话
一遍遍提醒那位青年，直到

that the woman's thane     for his father's deeds

2060   from blade's bite     blood-stained sleeps,

life forfeited;     him the other thence

escapes alive,     knows he the region well.

Then are broken     on both sides

sworn oaths of earls;     then in Ingeld

2065   will surge slaughter-hates,     and in him wife-love

after care's flood     cooler will become.

And so I Heatho-Bards'     loyalty not think,

treaty's portion,     is for Danes untreacherous,

friendship firm.     I shall further speak

2070   again of Grendel,     so that you well may know,

treasure-giver,     what then happened in

hand-clash of heroes.     When heaven's gem

had glided over earth,     guest angry came,

terrible, evening-grim,     us to seek,

2075   where we, unharmed,     hall guarded.

There was for Hondscio     battle fatal,

deathly for doomed man;     he first lay dead,

girded fighter;     for him Grendel was,

famed retainer,     the mouth-slayer,

2080   beloved man's     body all devoured.

Not the sooner out still     empty-handed

killer bloody-toothed,     slaughter-obsessed,

from the gold-hall     to go wished;

公主的扈从因父亲欠下的债

2060　倒在血泊里，利刃下送了性命。
　　　而那位凶手则逃之夭夭，因为
　　　在他自己的国家藏身方便。
　　　就这样，双方的誓约被打破，
　　　到时候英格德也会变得

2065　仇恨满腔，极大的悲愤促使他
　　　对妻子的爱恋渐渐淡忘。
　　　因此，我不相信希索巴人的诚意，
　　　不相信这联盟不带有欺骗，
　　　不相信他们能把友谊维持久长。①

2070　回头再说格兰道尔，我的恩主，
　　　您马上可以知道那场搏斗
　　　最后如何收场。当金乌西坠，
　　　那怒气冲冲的精灵乘着夜色
　　　偷偷前来袭击，而我们这班

2075　未曾受过伤害的人守卫着大厅。
　　　但武士汉德修却命运不济，
　　　他受到致命的攻击，最先
　　　丢了性命。这位著名的战士
　　　成了格兰道尔腹中之食，

2080　魔怪吞下了他整个躯体。
　　　满口血污的凶手不肯就此罢休，
　　　他存心毁灭一切，不甘心
　　　双手空空离开宴乐大厅。

① 贝奥武甫所说的这段历史当时尚未发生。

but he, for strength famed,    of me made trial,

2085    grasped with greedy hand.    Glove was hanging,

huge and strange,    with clasps secured;

it was deviously    all devised

from devil's crafts    and dragon's skins.

He me there inside,    unsinning,

2090    fierce deed-doer,    to stuff wished,

of many one;    it not he could so,

when I in anger    upright stood.


Too long is to tell    how I the people's scourge,

for evils all,    requital paid;

2095    there I, chieftain mine,    your people

honoured by acts.    He away got loose,

for a little while    life-ease enjoyed;

yet him the right,    his mark,remained,

hand in Heorot,    and he wretched thence,

2100    at heart gloomy,    to lake-depth sank.

Me for the death-clash    friend of Scyldings

with plated gold    plenty rewarded,

with many treasures,    when morning came,

and we to feast    sat down had.

2105    There was song and merriment;    old Scylding,

steeped in learning    from long ago told stories;

sometimes this warrior    harp for pleasure

力大无穷的他于是来考验我，

2085 贪婪地把我抓住。他的大手套<sup>①</sup>
高高悬垂，他的魔爪坚硬有力。
那手套采用妖法和龙皮缝制，
皱巴巴的显得奇异无比。
穷凶极恶的魔鬼无缘无故

2090 想把我装进他的手套里。
我怒不可遏，一骨碌坐起，
使他险恶的目的不能得逞。


至于我如何向他讨还血债，
如果一一叙说，未免啰唆。

2095 总之，我的主公，我为您的人民
赢得了荣誉。最后他脱身而走，
但他在这世上已活不长久。
他的右臂作为他的罪证
留在了鹿厅。他狼狈遁逸，

2100 绝望地钻进深深的潭底。
第二天上午，我们在鹿厅举宴，
希尔德子孙的朋友慷慨大方
为这场你死我活的血战
赏给我许多金银财宝。

2105 席间歌乐齐鸣，一片欢腾。
一位博识的老者讲起故事。
这位老战士时而拨动欢乐的竖琴，

① 手套，神话传说中巨人擒敌的法宝。

179

glee-wood strummed,      sometimes song recited,

true and tragic,      sometimes strange tales

2110   narrated rightly     open-hearted king;

sometimes again began,     by age knotted,

ancient warrior     youth to lament,

battle-strength;    heart within welled-up,

when he, with winters wise,    much remembered.

2115    So we there within     whole long day

pleasure took,    until night came

another to men.    Then was again swiftly

ready for grief-revenge    Grendel's mother,

set out sorrowful;    son death had snatched,

2120   war-hate of Wederas.    Woman monstrous

her child avenged,    warrior killed

savagely;    there was from Æschere,

wise old counsellor,    life departed.

Nor they him not could,    when morning came,

2125   death-weary,   Danes' people

in fire cremate    nor on pyre place

beloved man;    she the corpse carried off

in foe's embrace    under mountain stream.

That was for Hrothgar    sorrow bitterest

2130   which the people's leader    long had suffered.

Then the king me,    by your life,

implored in anguish    that I in waters' throng

时而唱起真实而悲伤的歌，

有板有眼地叙述奇闻逸事，

2110　以及心胸豁达的国王的事迹。

有时候这位年迈的武士

还怀念起他自己青年时代

在战场上的神勇。回顾已逝的岁月，

年迈的智者禁不住心潮澎湃！

2115　就这样，我们快活地度过

漫长的白昼，直到另一个黑夜

降临人间。然后是格兰道尔的母亲

踏上不幸的旅程，急切为

重伤的儿子报仇。她的儿子，

2120　高特人的仇敌已被死亡虏获。

女魔为报仇残杀了一位武士：

那人名叫伊斯切尔，他是宫中

年迈而聪慧的议事大臣。

第二天，丹麦人无法把他火化，

2125　无法把这位叮敬的长者

抬上柴堆，因为女魔劫掠了

他的尸体，早已返回深山，

潜入水中洞府。赫罗斯加国王

经受过的磨难数不胜数，

2130　但这一次使他感到最痛苦。

苦恼的国王因此恳求我，

要我看在您的面上进入激流，

heroic act achieved,     life risked,

glory accomplished;    he me rewards promised.

2135  I then the maelstrom's,    as is widely known,

grim ghastly    depth-guard found.

There us a while was    hand with hand locked;

water with gore welled,    and I head cut off

in the war-hall    of Grendel's mother

2140  with huge sword;    not easily thence

life I brought back;    not was I doomed yet;

but me heroes' keeper    again handed

treasures many,    son of Halfdane.


So the tribe-king    honourably lived;

2145  by no means I the gifts    forgone had,

strength's reward,    but he me treasures gave,

son of Halfdane,    of my own choice;

these I to you, warrior king,    to bring wish,

graciously offer.    Still is all in you

2150  favours' fount;    I few have

close kinsmen    besides, Hygelac, you."

Ordered then in to bring    boar-crested standard,

battle-steep helmet,    grey byrnie,

war-sword glorious;    tale again took up:

2155    "Me this battle-gear    Hrothgar gave,

wise ruler;    with some words he ordered

再次建功立业，冒着生命危险
争取荣光。他还答应给我重赏。

2135　我于是钻进深潭，去寻找
凶恶的魔主，这事人人都已知晓。
我们当时徒手格斗了很久；
鲜血染红了潭水，争战中
我得到一把巨剑，砍下了

2140　格兰道尔母亲的头颅。我能活着回来，
并非轻而易举。是我命不该绝。
王公的保护人，哈夫丹的儿子
于是又赏我许多金银财物。


丹麦王从此得以高枕无忧，

2145　而我则得到应得的报酬。
哈夫丹的儿子慷慨大方，
任凭我挑选他的全部宝藏。
伟大的主公，我把礼物全献给您，
以表我的心意。您的仁慈

2150　就是我的依傍，海格拉克啊，
除了您我已没有别的亲人。"
他命人抬进一面饰有野猪头的战旗、
一顶高冠的头盔、一副铁灰的胸甲、
一把漂亮的宝剑，并接着说：

2155　"英明的赫罗斯加赏我这副盔甲，
他还有话要我向您转达：

that I its first you      ancestry should tell;

said that it had      Heorogar king,

leader of Scyldings,      long while;

2160    not the sooner to son his      leave he would,

to bold Heoroweard,      though he to him loyal was,

breast-armour.      Use it all well."

     Heard I that with the treasures      four horses,

swift, all alike,      behind followed,

2165    apple-yellow;      he him gifts offered,

horses and riches.      So shall kinsman act,

not malice-nets      for others weave

with secret cunning,      death contrive

of close companions.      To Hygelac was,

2170    in battle fierce,      nephew very loyal,

and each the other's      benefit remembered.

     Heard I that he the neck-ring      to Hygd presented,

exquisite marvel-jewel      which him Wealhtheow gave,

chieftain's daughter,      three horses too,

2175    supple and saddle-bright;      her then was,

after ring-accepting,      breast adorned.

     Thus showed boldness,      son of Ecgtheow,

man for combats famed,      for good deeds,

acted for honour;      never, drunk, slew

2180    hearth-companions;      was not him cruel heart,

but he mankind's      greatest strength,

这件宝物还有一段来历

它当初一直为希罗加国王①,

丹麦人的统帅所有,但他没有把它

2160　传给自己的儿子希罗窝德,尽管

他的儿子对他一直忠诚。

因此,请您务必加倍珍惜。"

我②还听说除了这批财物

还有四匹骏马,匹匹善于奔跑,

2165　长一身栗色皮毛。他把良驹和财宝

全献给了国王。亲人之间

本来就应该这样,万万不可

明争暗斗,编织仇恨的罗网,

置对方于死地。在激烈的战斗中

2170　他对海格拉克赤胆忠心,

这舅甥俩始终相互照应。

我听说他还把那个硕大的项圈,

维瑟欧所赠的稀世之宝,连同

三匹鞍鞯闪闪发光的骏马,转赠

2175　希格德王后。她收下这份厚礼,

即刻把项圈挂在自己胸前。

就这样,艾克塞奥之子大显神威,

战场上名声远场,他的言行举止

人人称赞;他从不会酒后胡作非为,

2180　杀害亲密的伙伴。他有仁慈的心肠,

拥有上帝赋予的慷慨礼物,

① 即赫罗斯加
的哥哥。

② 诗人自己。

185

generous gift,     which him God gave,

kept, battle-brave.     Humble had been for long,

so him Geats' sons     good not reckoned,

2185  nor him on mead-bench     much honour

lord of Wederas     grant would;

strongly thought     that he slack was,

youth unambitious.     About-turn came

to glory-favoured man     for misfortunes all.

2190     Ordered then heroes' keeper     in to be fetched,

battle-brave king,     Hrethel's heirloom,

gold-adorned;     was not among Geats then

rich treasure better     in sword's shape;

that he in Beowulf's     lap laid,

2195  and him gave     seven thousand hides of land,

hall and high-seat.     Theirs was both together

in that nation     land inherited,

earth by odal right;     to one alone belonged

broad kingdom,     he who there lordlier was.

沙场上英勇无比,他的勇力
盖世无双。只可惜他长期被埋没,
高特人并没有把他当作勇士,
2185　在宴乐大厅,高特的国王
也从未向他颁发过荣誉的奖赏。
他们固执地怀疑他懒散成性,
胸无大志。如今时来运转,
往昔的困厄终于一去不返。

2190　然后,王公的保护者吩咐下人
拿来他父亲雷塞尔传下的宝物,
一柄镶金古剑。在高特人中间,
没有人拥有过如此珍贵的兵器。
他把宝剑放在贝奥武甫膝盖上,
2195　还赏了他采邑几十万亩,
包括宴乐厅和宝座。他们两人
都合法继承了祖辈的产业;
不过,他们中更其高贵的一位
继承的是一个辽阔的王国。

# PART TEN
## Beowulf and the Dragon

2200 In time it turned out in later days

in battle-clashes, when Hygelac lay dead

and to Heardred war-blades

under shield-cover death caused,

when him sought out in victory-tribe,

2205 hard war-fighters, Battle-Scylfings,

in force they attacked nephew of Hereric:

then to Beowulf broad kingdom

in hand passed; he held it well

fifty winters, was then wise king,

2210 old land-warden, until one began

in dark nights dragon to rule,

he who on high heath hoard guarded,

stone-barrow steep; path below lay

to men unknown. There inside went

2215 of man some kind who close approached

to heathen hoard; hand cup took,

large, gem-adorned; not he it then hid

that he sleeping tricked had been

by thief's craft; it the people found,

# 十

## 贝奥武甫与火龙

2200　光阴荏苒,海格拉克国王
　　　阵亡在疆场,随后那战刀
　　　又劈开赫德莱德①的坚盾,　　　　　　　① 海格拉克的
　　　好勇斗狠的瑞典人一路追击,　　　　　　　儿子。
　　　在这光荣之国,残忍地杀害
2205　赫莱里克②的外甥——从那以后,　　② 王后希格德
　　　这幅员辽阔的高特王国　　　　　　　　　的兄弟,赫德莱
　　　就全归贝奥武甫一人当政。　　　　　　　德的舅父。
　　　他成功地治理这个国家,
　　　达五十个春秋,他是一位明主,
2210　王国的老卫士,直到一条火龙
　　　趁着黑夜胡作非为,那孽障
　　　出没在荒野,盘踞于陡峭的石冢,
　　　守护着一笔宝藏。那地方
　　　只通一条无人知晓的小径。
2215　然而,却有人(顺着小径进入
　　　这异教的宝库,偷走一只
　　　镶有珠宝的金杯。火龙不再沉默,
　　　尽管它当时呼呼入睡,上了
　　　窃贼的当,但邻近的居民发现,

2220   neighbours of men,     that he enraged was.


     Not at all with intent     serpent-hoard broke

     of his own will     he who him sorely harmed,

     but for dire need     a slave of some

     men's sons     hate-blows fled,

2225   of refuge needy,     and there inside went,

     man crime-guilty.     At once

     that... to the stranger     shock-terror stood;

     yet wretched     ..........

     ..........     ........shaped

2230   .........     when him the shock seized,

     treasure-cup...     There were such many

     in the earth-house     ancient treasures,

     as them in yore-days     man unknown

     huge legacy     of noble kin,

2235   wise-thinking     there hid,

     costly treasures.     All them death took

     in former times,     and the one then yet

     of tribe's retainers     who there longest lived,

     guardian friend-grieving,     expected the same,

2240   that he little time     long-got treasure

     enjoy might.     Barrow all-ready

     stood on plain     to water-waves near,

     new by ness,     by skill-crafts secured;

2220 这火龙早已恼怒得七窍生烟。)①

其实,那位侵犯了火龙的人
并非存心要潜入龙窟盗宝。
他只是出于无奈,因为他
是某人的奴隶,为逃避主子的鞭笞

2225 误入龙窟避难。有罪的人
走进洞里,突然间发现火龙,
心中不由得升起一阵惶恐;
可怜的罪人……
……形状如……

2230 ……惊慌失措中
拿了一只金杯。②这样的古珍
洞窟中不计其数。看样子,
古时候有个不知姓名的人
经过深思熟虑选中此地

2235 藏匿某个高贵部落的巨额遗产。
死神早早夺走族人的性命,
最后只剩下那位藏宝的人,
他活得最久,悲伤地悼念
他的朋友,但他心里清楚

2240 他自己也来日无多,世代积聚的财富
他已无缘消受。天然的古冢
坐落在波涛汹涌的海岸上,
依傍着岩岬,入口处十分隐蔽。

① 这一部分原稿残缺严重,括号中的内容只是后人的猜测。

② 原文有数行文字缺失。

191

there inside bore     of noble treasures

2245    rings' warden     hoard-worthy part,

of plated gold,     few words spoke:

     "Hold you now, earth,     now heroes not may,

earls' possessions!     Well, it formerly from you

good men obtained;     war-death took off,

2250    life-murder terrible,     of men each

of people my    who this life gave up;

they had seen hall-joy.     I have none who sword might wield

or polish     plated flagon,

drink-cup precious;     retinue elsewhere departed.

2255    Shall the hard helmet,     adorned with gold,

of ornaments be stripped;     burnishers slumber,

those who battle-masks    prepare should;

also the war-mail,     which in combat felt

among shields' crash     the bite of irons,

2260    decays after warrior.     Not may byrnie's ring

with war-fighter    widely fare,

heroes beside.    Not was harp's joy,

delight of glee-wood,     not good hawk

through hall swoops,     not the swift horse

2265    courtyard tramps.    Baleful death has

many of living-kins    forth sent."

     So, sad-minded,    in sorrow he moaned

alone after all,    unhappy passed

财宝的主人把能藏匿的部分，

2245　包括各种金制器皿，一一搬进洞里，
　　　然后他悲伤地说了几句话：
　　　"大地呀，人留不住王公的财产，
　　　如今请你妥善保存吧！这一切
　　　本来都从你身上取得；战争的屠杀

2250　剥夺了我同胞的性命，他们一个个
　　　奔赴黄泉，抛弃了人间欢乐，
　　　从此再没有人来挥舞这里的剑，
　　　再没有人把这镶金嵌银的酒盅
　　　擦得锃亮。王公贵族都已各奔东西。

2255　坚固的头盔，尽管镶有黄金，
　　　仍会失去光泽；原先擦拭它的人
　　　早已安静地长眠在地下。
　　　战场上经受刀枪撕咬的胸甲
　　　也一样命运不济，主人一死，

2260　它也随即腐朽。盔甲上的金环
　　　难以再伴随出征的英雄
　　　周游世界。再听不见竖琴的欢唱，
　　　再没有乐器的奏鸣，再没有温顺的猎鹰
　　　穿梭在厅堂，再没有日行万里的骏马

2265　溜达在庭院。可恨的死神
　　　打发了无数部落的芸芸众生。"
　　　就这样，他哀诉着自己的痛苦，
　　　孑然一身，在不幸中度过日日夜夜，

through day and night    until death's flood

2270   touched at heart.    Hoard-joy found

old dawn-destroyer    open standing,

he who, burning,    barrows seeks,

naked foe-dragon,    by night flies

in fire enfolded;    him land-dwellers

2275   greatly dread.    He seek out must

hoard in earth    where he heathen gold

guards, in winters wise;    not is for him any the better.

Thus the tribe-smasher    three hundred winters

held in earth    of hoard-caves one,

2280   vastly strong,    until him one angered

man in heart;    to liege-lord bore

plated cup,    for truce-pact begged

lord his.    Then was hoard plundered,

borne off rings' hoard,    boon granted

2285   to wretched man;    lord examined

men's ancient work    for first time.

Then the worm awoke,    war was renewed;

slid then over stone,    strong-hearted found

foe's foot-print;    he too far had stepped

2290   in secret cunning    to dragon's head near.

Thus may, undoomed,    easily survive

woe and exile-grief,    he whom Ruler's

grace protects.    Hoard-guard sought

直到有一天，死亡的洪流

2270 淹没他的心房。这笔无人看管的宝藏
后来被黑夜的偷袭者发现，
可恶的火龙到处寻找洞穴，
喷吐着火焰在夜间飞行；
当地居民见了无不胆战心惊。

2275 正是它找到了这个宝库，
于是年复一年看护起异教的财富。
这差事对于它倒也合适有度。
三百个春秋过去，这生灵的摧残者，
强大的庞然怪物，一直守护着

2280 这地下的宝库，直到有人
把它激怒。盗宝者把那只金杯
献给了他的主人，以求他的宽恕。
宝藏就这样遭到世人的光顾，
金杯被窃走，那可怜的人

2285 因此获得恩典。他的主人
也是首次见识这件古代奇珍；
毒龙一觉醒来，战祸即刻降临。
阴险凶狠的恶魔爬出石壁，
探察仇敌的足迹。当初盗贼小心翼翼

2290 竟然从火龙眼皮底下溜之大吉。
命不该绝的人显然有主的庇护，
即使经历大灾难，也能安然无恙。
宝库的守护者早已迫不及待，

eagerly over ground,     wished man to find
2295  who him in sleep     sorely treated;
hot and fierce-hearted     mound often circled
all outward;     not there any man
in the wasteland,     yet in war he rejoiced,
in battle's action;     at times to barrow turned,
2300  rich-cup sought;     he soon found
that had man one     gold disturbed,
noble treasure.     Hoard-guard waited,
impatiently,     until evening came,
was then enraged     barrow's keeper,
2305  wished the foe     with flame to repay
drink-cup precious.     Then was day vanished,
to snake's delight;     not on wall longer
to wait wished,     but amid flame fared,
by fire im pelled.     Was the onset terrible
2310  for folk in land;     so it soon was
for their wealth-giver     in agony ended.

Then the stranger began     flames to spew,
bright homes to burn;     blaze-light rose,
to men's horror;     not there anything alive
2315  evil air-flier     leave would.
Was the worm's war-strength     widely seen,
cruel foe's malice     from near and far,

196

决意查个水落石出,找到那个

2295　趁它熟睡时掠夺龙窟的盗贼。
　　　它暴跳如雷,不时地在洞府周围
　　　兜来转去。但荒野中见不到
　　　任何人影。它已横下一条心,
　　　决意以战为乐。它一次次折回洞府,

2300　寻找那只金杯。它终于恍然大悟:
　　　有人已动过它的金库,盗走了
　　　稀世之珍。宝藏的卫士恨不得
　　　夜幕即刻降临;石冢的主人
　　　早已怒不可遏,它渴望着

2305　以复仇的烈焰讨还珍贵的金杯。
　　　白昼终于过去,毒龙喜不自胜;
　　　它不愿继续等待在陡峭的石壁,
　　　它要即刻出发,喷吐熊熊的火焰,
　　　踏上征程。这最初的景象

2310　令当地人毛骨悚然,后来的结局
　　　对财宝的赐予者是莫大的悲伤。


　　　恶魔于是开始喷吐火焰,
　　　烧着了房屋;只见火光冲天,
　　　村民们惊恐万状。可怕的飞龙

2315　存心毁灭一切活着的生灵。
　　　毒龙的暴行已经有目共睹,
　　　它把仇恨随处散布,战争的凶顽

how the war-destroyer     Geats' folk

hated and harmed;     to hoard back hurried,

2320   to lord-hall hidden,     before day's time.

He had land-dwellers     in flame enfolded,

in blaze and burning;     barrow he trusted,

war-strength and wall;     him this faith deceived.

Then was to Beowulf     terror made known

2325   quickly in truth,     that his own home,

of buildings finest,     in burn-swells melted,

gift-seat of Geats.     That to the good man was

misery in heart,     of mind-sorrows greatest;

thought the wise warrior     that he Ruler

2330   against old law     eternal Lord

bitterly had angered;     breast within welled

with dark thoughts,     as for him usual not was.

Had flame-dragon     folk's fortress,

coastal lands,     stronghold the

2335   with fire destroyed;     him for it war-king,

Wederas' chief,     revenge devised.

Ordered for him then to make,     warriors' protector,

all-iron,     earls' over-lord,

war-shield awesome:     knew he well

2340   that him tree-wood     help not could,

linden against flame.     Must loaned-days'

noble old-good     end abide,

向高特的黎民百姓发泄怨毒,

造成伤害。每当天色放明,

2320 它又急急返回自己的巢穴。

它用熊熊燃烧的火舌包围

当地的居民。它自恃威力无比,

所造壁垒森严,其实它在欺骗自己。

贝奥武甫很快见识了这种恐怖:

2325 他自己的家园,那雄伟的厅堂,

高特人的宫廷,也被大火吞没。

仁慈的国王痛心疾首,他的悲哀

比谁的都深沉。智慧的武士

以为自己冒犯了永恒的主,

2330 违背了上帝规定的戒律。

他的胸中涌起阴郁的思绪,

这在他生平还是第一次。

怒气冲天的毒龙用大火

摧毁高特人的城堡、沿海的土地。

2335 战争的统帅,百姓的明主,

决心为此向火龙报仇雪耻。

武士的庇护人,贵族的领袖,

首先命人用上等的钢铁

为他铸造一面坚固的盾牌。

2340 他心里十分清楚,林中的木头

经不起烈焰的燃烧。仁慈的国王

总有寿终正寝的一天,尘世的生命

world's life,      and the worm together,

although hoard-wealth      he held for long.

2345      Scorned then      rings' ruler

that he the wide-flier      with troop attacked,

with farge force;      not he for him the strife feared,

nor for him the serpent's power      at all respected,

strength and courage,      because he already many,

2350   peril daring,      hostilities survived,

battle-clashes,      since he Hrothgar's,

victory-favoured man,      hall purged,

and in combat death-gripped      Grendel's race,

loathed kindred.      Not the least was

2355   of hand-encounters      where Hygelac was slain,

when Geats' king      in war's onslaughts,

lord-friend of folk      Frisia-lands in,

Hrethel's heir      in sword-drink died,

by blade down-beaten.      Thence Beowulf came

2360   by self's strength,      swim-feat achieved;

had him on arm      earls' thirty

battle-trappings      when he to sea plunged.

Not at all the Hetware      to be exultant needed

over foot-fight,      who him forth against

2365   shields bore;      few back came

from the warrior      home to visit.

Overswam then sea's expanse      son of Ecgtheow,

乃租赁之物,拥有宝藏的毒龙

与他一样无法摆脱死亡的命运。

2345 项圈的赐予者准备与飞龙作战,

但他不屑于动用浩荡的大军。

他自己并不害怕搏杀,并未

把威力无穷的大蛇放在眼里。

因为他早已久经沙场,自从

2350 他为赫罗斯加的大厅肃清

魔怪的祸患,搏杀中杀死

格兰道尔,灭其可恶的一族,

胜利的武士九死一生,经历过

无数次战斗的考验。想当年

2355 海格拉克,高特人的国王,

百姓高贵的恩主,雷塞尔的儿子

在弗罗西亚人疾风骤雨般的攻击中

死于非命,倒在战刀底下,

那次血战非同寻常。贝奥武甫

2360 凭自己的神力和水性得以生还,

当他返身跃入大海,肩膀上

还扛了三十副缴获的铠甲。

当希特威尔人①持盾与他徒步厮杀

他们没有理由吹嘘自己:

2365 因为从他手中逃得性命

重返家园的人寥寥无几。

艾克塞奥之子终于游过茫茫大海,

① 与弗罗西亚人结盟的一个部落。

201

wretched solitary      back to tribe;

there him Hygd offered      wealth and kingdom,

2370    rings and royal-seat;      in son not she trusted,

that he against foreign armies      native thrones

hold could,      then was Hygelac dead.

Not the sooner unhappy men      find could

in the noble Beowulf      any way

2375    that he to Heardred      lord would be,

or the kingdom      choose would;

yet he him among folk      with friendly counsels upheld,

kindly with favour,      until he older grew,

Weder-Geats ruled.      Him exile-men

2380    across sea sought,      sons of Ohthere;

had they rebelled against      helm of Scylfings,

the finest      of sea-kings

who in Sweden      wealth dispensed,

famed chieftain.      For Heardred it as end came;

2385    he there for hospitality      death-wound received

from sword's strokes,      son of Hygelac;

and back went      Ongentheow's son

home to seek,      when Heardred lay dead,

let the royal-seat      Beowulf hold,

2390    Geats to rule;      that was good king.

He for chief's fall      revenge remembered

孑然一身回到他的同胞中间。

希格德王后把宝库和王国,

2370　项圈和御座都交到他手里。

她信不过自己的儿子,海格拉克死后,

她担心儿子不能坐稳江山,抵御外敌。

然而,高尚的贝奥武甫无论如何

不肯满足丧亲者的请求,他不愿

2375　取代赫德莱德登上王座,

接受国王的权柄。相反,

他极力扶持王子,友善地

辅佐他,尊敬他,直到他成年,

有能力自己治理这个国家。

2380　后来,欧赛尔的两个儿子被流放,①

渡海来到高特王国。他俩背叛了

瑞典人的保护者,那位海内

最著名的国王,分赐财富的恩主。

此事导致赫德莱德命赴黄泉:

2385　海格拉克的儿子殷勤好客,

却被利剑刺中,受了致命伤。

赫德莱德一死,奥根索的儿子②

返回自己的家园,于是贝奥武甫

登上宝座,开始治理高特王国。

2390　他不愧为一个英明的国王!


他一直不忘为已故的国王报仇,

① 欧赛尔继承奥根索的王位,成为瑞典的国王。他死后,其兄弟奥尼拉篡夺王位,并流放了欧赛尔的两个儿子伊恩蒙德和伊吉尔斯。两位王子到高特避难,赫德莱德收留了他们,结果招来杀身之祸。

② 指奥尼拉。

203

in later days,      to Eadgils he became

in misery friend;     with army he supported

over lake broad     son of Ohthere,

2395   with warriors and weapons;    Eadgils took revenge then

in cold grief-forays;    king Onela of life he deprived.

    So he enmities all    survived had,

cruel conflicts,    son of Ecgtheow,

courage-deeds,    until the one day

2400   when he with serpent    struggle must.

Went then, of twelve one,    with anger swollen,

lord of Geats,    dragon to face;

had then heard    whence the feud arose,

fierce hate for men;    him to bosom came

2405   treasure-cup famous    by the finder's hand.

He was in that group    thirteenth man,

who this strife's    onset caused,

captive heart-sad,    must unhappy thence

the place point out.    He against will went

2410   to where he earth-hall    alone knew,

barrow under ground    to sea-surge near,

to wave-strife;    it was inside full

of jewels and golden coils.    Warden monstrous,

wary war-fighter,    gold treasures guarded

2415   old under earth;    was not that easy bargain

to obtain    for man any.

后来他与绝望中的伊吉尔斯

交了朋友。他派出自己的武士

带上武器援助欧赛尔之子

2395　跨过大海;经过悲壮的远征,

伊吉尔斯报了仇,奥尼拉丢了性命。

就这样,艾克塞奥之子经历了

一场场战斗,一回回冒险,

一次次壮举,直到有一天

2400　他必须与大蛇性命相拼。

义愤填膺的国王于是带上

十一名战士去寻找火龙。

他此时已知道血仇的起因,

仇恨的根源。那只金光闪闪的金杯

2405　已从盗宝者手中转到他那里。

那个肇事者加入了征讨的行列,

成了队伍中第十三人。可怜的奴隶

心情沮丧,但他必须作为向导

去寻找龙窟。他很不情愿在前带路,

2410　奔向只有他知道的地下大厅,

那座与汹涌的海浪毗邻的石冢。

那里面藏着无数金银珠宝。

凶恶的保护者正严阵以待,

捍卫着这古老的地下宝库。

2415　不管是谁都别想轻而易举

从他那里得到这笔丰厚的财富。

Sat then on headland     fight-hard king,

while good-luck wished     to hearth-companions,

gold-friend of Geats.     Him was sad heart,

2420    restless and slaughter-keen,     fate all too near

which the old man     greet must,

seek soul's treasure,     asunder sever

life from limb;     not then for long was

life of chief     in flesh enwrapped.

2425    Beowulf spoke,     son of Ecgtheow:

"Many I in youth     war-storms survived,

battle-times;     I it all remember.

I was seven winters     when me treasures' prince,

lord-friend of people,     from my father took;

2430    held me and kept me     Hrethel king,

gave me wealth and feasting,     kinship recalled;

not was I by him in life     less loved in aught,

warrior in stronghold,     than of his sons each,

Herebeald and Hæthcyn     or Hygelac my.

2435    Was for the eldest     unfittingly

by kinsman's acts     a death-bed strewed,

when him Hæthcyn     from horn-bow

his lord-friend     with arrow struck down,

missed mark     and his kinsman shot,

2440    one brother the other     with bloody bolt.

That was irreparable assault,     heinously sinned,

骁勇善战的国王在石崖上坐下，

高特人赐金的朋友向他的亲信

表达良好的祝愿。他心情沉重，

2420　预感死亡就在眼前，命运之神

已靠近这位皓首老人，将夺取

他的灵魂，存心把他的生命

从躯壳中分离。高尚的人

有生的时日已经屈指可数。

2425　艾克塞奥之子贝奥武甫说：

"我年轻时经历过无数次争战，

这一切我至今记忆犹新。

当我七岁时，财富的主人，

百姓的明主把我领出家门，

2430　雷塞尔国王收养我，抚养我，

他看重亲情，赐我财富与美食，

待我恩宠有加，在城堡中，

我被一视同仁，就像他亲生的儿子

赫巴德、赫斯辛和海格拉克。

2435　三兄弟中年长的一位死于非命，

造成不幸的却是自己的亲人：

当时赫斯辛拉开弯弯的长弓，

但他的箭没有射中目标，反而

击中了自己的同胞手足，

2440　亲人害了亲人，箭镞鲜血淋淋。

这致命的一箭正中心脏，

to heart mind-wearying;      must yet however

prince unavenged     from life depart.

    So too is sad    for old man

2445   to suffer    that his son rides

young on gallows;    then he dirge utters,

sorrowing song,    when his son hangs

for raven to relish,    and he him help not can,

old and knowing,    any provide.

2450   Always is reminded,    morning each,

of son's departure;    another not he cares

to wait for,    strongholds within,

inheritor,    when the one has

through death's compulsion    deeds fathomed.

2455   He sees, sorrow-caring,    in his son's house

wine-hall wasted,    windy rest-place

of joy bereft;    riders sleep,

heroes in grave;    not is there harp's sound,

gaiety in courts,    such as there once was.


2460    Goes then to bed,    sorrow-dirge sings

one living for one dead;    seemed to him all too roomy

fields and dwelling-place.    Thus Wederas' leader

for Herebeald    heart's sorrow

seething suffered;    at all not could

2465   on the life-slayer    feud avenge;

再也无法补救,好端端一位王子

无端丧生,又无从报仇雪恨。

国王好不悲伤,他像一个老人

2445　眼睁睁看着自己的儿子

上了绞刑架,唯有哀叹,唯有悲吟,

儿子的尸体高高挂起,成了

乌鸦的美食,白发苍苍的他

却想不出任何办法帮助自己。

2450　每天早晨,他总免不了要怀念

去世的儿子。他已无心等待

另一个继承人长大成人,因为

他的长子已被死神征服,

走完了他生命的全部旅程。

2455　他满怀忧伤,眼巴巴看着

儿子住过的大厅空空荡荡,

风雨潇潇,一片凄凉。骑士睡着了,

战士已入黄土。厅堂里从此

再听不见竖琴欢快的乐音。


2460　活着的为死去的唱着哀歌,

返回自己的卧室。在他眼里

田野和居室都显得过于空旷。

就这样,高特国王因赫巴德的死

内心充满无限的悲哀,然而,

2465　他又不能向凶手讨还血债。

nor the more he the warrior     hound not might

with hostile acts,     though Hæthcyn by him loved not was.

He then with the sorrow     that on him sorely fell,

human-joys gave up,     God's light he chose;

2470     to heirs left,     as does happy man,

land and tribe-fort     when he from life went.

     Then was struggle and strife     of Swedes and Geats,

across wide water     warfare shared,

hostility hard,     when Hrethel died,

2475     and Ongentheow's     heirs were

bold, pugnacious,     peace not would

across lakes hold,     but around Hreosnabeorh

dreadful savage slaughter     often wrought.

That kin-friends     my avenged,

2480     feud and falsity,     as it famous was,

though one with his     life paid,

hard bargain;     for Hæthcyn was,

for Geats' lord,     conflict fatal.

Then I in morning heard     one kinsman other

2485     with blade's edges     on slayer avenge,

where Ongentheow     Eofor attacks;

war-helm he split,     aged Scylfing Ongentheow

fell, sword-pale;     hand remembered

feuds a-plenty,     death-stroke not withheld.

2490     I him the treasures     which Hygelac me gave

尽管他向来不喜欢赫斯辛，

　　但他不能怀着仇恨将他伤害。

　　身心所承受的痛苦实在太多，

　　他宁愿放弃人间欢乐，选择上帝的光明。

2470　他终于像一个幸福者告别人生，

　　把土地和城堡留给了子孙。

　　雷塞尔死后，瑞典和高特之间

　　爆发了战争和冲突，两个部落

　　在茫茫大海上争斗，发泄仇恨。

2475　奥根索的儿子一个个好勇斗狠，

　　不愿大海两岸出现和平。

　　他们常常在希罗斯纳堡一带

　　制造阴险而野蛮的屠杀。

　　我的舅父偿还了血仇与罪行，

2480　这事大家都已知道，然而，

　　他们中的一位为此付出了性命，

　　那代价真够惨重。赫斯辛，

　　高特人的国王①阵亡在战场。

　　我听说次日清晨，当奥根索

2485　大战奥佛尔，我的另一位舅父①

　　用宝剑向他讨还了血债：

　　头盔被砍破，年迈的奥根索

　　受了致命伤。他死有余辜，

　　因为他的手早已沾满血腥。

2490　而我在战场上则顺应命运，

① 赫斯辛误杀了自己的兄弟，其父雷塞尔因伤心过度，不久亡故，这以后便由赫斯辛继承王位。

① 即海格拉克。

repaid in battle,      as me granted was,

with shining sword;      he me land gave,

earth, odal-joy.      Was not for him any need

that he among Gifthas      or Spear-Danes

2495    or in Swedes' kingdom      to seek needed

a worse war-fighter,      with wealth buy him;

always I him in troop      before would go,

alone in vanguard,      and thus always shall

in battle act      while this sword lasts,

2500    which me, early and late,      often served,

since I, before the retinues,      of Dæghrefn was

the hand-slayer,      of Franks' champion.

No way he the spoils      to Frisian king,

breast-adorning,      to bring was able,

2505    but in battle fell      banner's keeper,

the noble in courage;      not was blade the killer,

but him my battle-grip      heart's surges,

bone-house, broke.      Now must blade's edge,

hand and hard sword,      for hoard contend."

用明晃晃的宝剑报答了海格拉克
赐我黄金的恩情。他给了我土地
和幸福的家园。因此他用不着再到
基夫塞人、丹麦人或瑞典人中间

2495　花费他的金银财宝,招募
远不如我的武士。战场上,
我总是在前面冲锋陷阵,
做他的先锋。在我一生中,
我都如此拼杀在战场,只要

2500　这把跟随我作战多年的剑
能承受战争的考验,想当年
我曾在激战中杀死了达莱芬,
那位法兰克武士。他未能
将我的盔甲带给弗罗西亚国王,

2505　这位旗手,高贵的武士最终丧生
在沙场。当时我并未动用宝剑,
而是用我的铁掌撕断了
他的脊骨。但今天为了夺取宝藏,
我得把宝剑和铁掌都派上用场。”

# PART ELEVEN
## Beowulf Attacks the Dragon

2510  Beowulf spoke,  boast-words uttered

for last time:   "I tackled many

contests in youth;   even now I wish,

wise folk-guardian,   feud to seek,

glory to earn,   if me the evil ravager

2515  from earth-hall  out attacks."

  Greeted then  warriors each,

bold helm-bearers,   for final time,

close companions:   "Not would I sword bear,

weapon against serpent,   if I knew how

2520  with the monster  else I might

for glory grapple,   as I formerly with Grendel did;

but I there battle-fire's  heat expect,

breath and poison;   therefore I me on have

shield and byrnie.   Not will I barrow's guard

2525  flee one foot's pace,   but we further shall

fare at the wall  as us fate allots,

Maker of men all.   I am in mind so bold

that I against the war-flier  from boast abstain.

  Wait you on barrow  in byrnies clad,

# 十一
# 贝奥武甫战火龙

2510　贝奥武甫最后一次发出
　　　他的豪言壮语："我年轻时
　　　曾身经百战；如今年事已高，
　　　但作为人民的庇护者，只要作恶者
　　　胆敢从地洞里爬出，我就一定

2515　向他挑战，让我的英名千古流传。"
　　　然后，他最后一次逐一嘱咐
　　　勇敢的武士，他的亲密战友，
　　　他这样说："我不想使用刀枪
　　　对付那条长虫，如果除此之外

2520　还有别的办法，我会与他徒手相搏，
　　　就像当年与格兰道尔争战那样。
　　　但这一次我得防范熊熊的烈焰、
　　　沸腾的毒气，因此，我只得
　　　把自己披挂整齐。我不会

2525　在墓冢的守护者面前后退半步，
　　　我与它将遭遇在绝壁，一任
　　　命运的裁决。我对自己充满信心，
　　　用不着与人联手战胜顽敌。
　　　请你们披盔戴甲全副武装，

2530    warriors in war-gear,     to see which better may

after death-clash     wound survive

of us two.     Not is it your venture,

nor in power of man,     save mine alone,

that he against monster     strength should pit,

2535    heroic deed achieve.     I with courage shall

gold gain,     or war will take,

life-murder terrible,     lord your."

    Arose then by shield     bold warrior,

hard under helm,     sword-sark wore

2540    under stone-cliffs,     strength he trusted

of single man;     not is such coward's way.

Saw then by wall     —he who very many,

ungrudgingly good,     struggles survived,

battle-combats,     when clash armies—

2545    standing stone-arch,     stream out thence

bursting from barrow;     was the brook's surge

with deadly fire hot,     not he could by hoard near

unburning     any while

the depth endure     for dragon's flame.

2550    Let then from breast,     when he angered was,

Weder-Geats' leader     word out fare,

strong at heart he shouted;     voice in went

battle-clear ringing     under hoary stone.

Hate was aroused,     hoard-guard knew

2530　等待在墓冢边,看看血战之后
　　　我和它谁能保住自己的性命。
　　　这次冒险你们不必参与,
　　　除了我自己,任何人都用不着
　　　为了人间的荣耀跟这恶魔

2535　斗力争胜。我有勇气去夺取
　　　金银财宝,否则就让可怕的血战
　　　使你们失去自己的国王。"
　　　说完,勇敢的武士站起身,
　　　他手持坚盾,头戴钢盔,身穿铠甲

2540　来到悬崖底下,他深信自己的力量,
　　　他的行为与懦夫毫不相干——
　　　他经历过无数次战斗,枪林箭雨
　　　磨砺了他坚强的意志——此时,
　　　他抬头观看,只见悬崖中

2545　出现一个洞穴,一股水流
　　　从里面涌出;湍流中弥漫着
　　　致命的烈焰,他无法接近
　　　那个宝库,因为毒龙的烈火
　　　能顷刻间烧毁周遭的一切。

2550　高特人的首领义愤填膺,
　　　禁不住从胸中发出一声怒吼,
　　　那叫阵的声音何其响亮,
　　　在灰色的岩壁上久久回荡。
　　　宝库的守护者听见人声,恼怒得

2555 man's voice;    not was there more time

for peace to plead.    Forth first came

breath of monster    out from stone,

hot battle-smoke;    earth thundered.

Fighter below barrow    shield-face turned

2560 against the terror-guest,    Geats' lord;

then was ring-coiled dragon's    heart impelled

strife to seek.    Sword before drew

good war-king,    ancient heirloom,

edges unblunt;    in each was

2565 of hostile-minded ones    horror of other.

Stout-hearted stood    by steep shield

friends' leader,    while the serpent coiled

swiftly together;    he in armour waited.

Went then burning    coiled slithering,

2570 to fate hastening.    Shield well protected

life and limb    for lesser while

famed chieftain,    than his mind desired,

where he that time    for first day

wield it must,    though him fate not assigned

2575 glory in battle.    Hand up raised

Geats' lord,    ghastly-hued dragon he struck

with old heirloom,    so that the edge gave way

bright on bone,    bit less sharply

than its tribe-king    need had,

2555 咬牙切齿。和平的光景从此
不复存在。魔怪张开大嘴
从石窟中喷出一股浓烟。
脚下的大地在震颤,墓冢下,
高特国王挥舞他的坚盾

2560 奋力抵抗可怕的客人。毒龙
蜷缩起身躯,早已急不可耐,
渴望屠戮生灵。英明的国王
拔剑出鞘,那祖传的宝贝
锋利无比。他们不共戴天,

2565 哪一方都严重威胁着对方的性命。
当大蛇迅速把身子蜷起,
人民的首领,意志坚强的国王,
把盾高高举起,随时准备进击。
毒龙在火焰中盘成一圈,

2570 随后便不顾死活向前猛扑。
坚固的盾保住了国王的性命,
但它的作用远不够令人称心。
国王平生第一次未能占得上风,
命运之神没有再赐予他

2575 胜利的光荣。高特人的国王
抬起手臂,用祖传的宝剑
砍向鳞光闪闪的长虫,但刀刃
在龙背上砸坏,在紧急关头,
这剑没有国王想象的那样锋利,

2580   in perils hard-pressed.    Then was barrow's guard

after battle-stroke    in baleful mood,

spewed death-fire;    widely sprang

battle-flames.    Of glory-victories not boasted

gold-friend of Geats;    war-blade failed

2585   naked in fight    as it not should,

iron old-good.    Not was it easy feat,

that the famed    son of Ecgtheow

earth-plain this    relinquish would;

must against will    in dwelling live

2590   elsewhere,    as must every man

take leave of loaned-days.    Was not then long to when

the awesome foes    each other again met.

Heartened him hoard-guard,    breast with breath swelled

a new time;    cruelly suffered

2595   in fire enfolded    he who once folk ruled.

Not at all him in group    hand-companions,

nobles' sons,    about took stand

in battle valour,    but they to wood slunk,

life to save.    Of them in one surged

2600   heart with sorrows;    kinship never can

aught be altered    for him who rightly thinks.


Wiglaf he was called,    Weohstan's son,

acclaimed shield-fighter,    man of Scylfings,

2580    没有砍进毒龙的躯体。
        宝库守护者被这一剑激怒,即刻喷吐
        置人于死地的火焰;熊熊的大火
        到处弥漫。高特人赐金的朋友
        再不能夸口胜利;他的宝剑

2585    已派不上用场,古代的利器
        本不该这样。这次征战未能如愿,
        大名鼎鼎的艾克塞奥之子
        并不愿从此离开他的土地。
        他心有不甘,但他必须迁居

2590    另一个地方,因为每个人
        都得把租赁的生命归还上帝。
        两个死对头紧接着再次交锋。
        宝藏的守护者振作精神,又吐出
        阵阵毒焰。曾经统治一方的国王

2595    被大火重重包围,痛苦万分。
        他那班随从,贵族的子孙,
        没有人敢鼓足勇气,与国王
        并肩作战,他们一溜烟逃进树林,
        只顾自己的性命。其中只有一人,

2600    对此极其悲愤,他为人正直,
        没有忘记自己与国王的亲情。


        他是威斯丹之子,名叫威格拉夫,
        一位来自瑞典的英勇武士,

kinsman of Ælfhere; saw his liege-lord

2605 under war-mask heat suffering.

Recalled then the honour that Beowulf him once gave,

home-land wealthy of Wægmundings,

folk-rights all, as his father had owned;

not could then hold back, hand shield seized,

2610 yellow linden, ancient sword drew;

it was among men Eanmund's legacy,

son of Ohthere; of Eanmund in battle was,

of exile friendless, Weohstan slayer

with sword's edges, and to Onela he brought

2615 bright-gleaming helm, ringed byrnie,

old sword of giant make; it to him Onela gave back,

his kinsman's war-clothing,

armour eager; not of the feud spoke,

though he his brother's son had slain.

2620 He the riches held for many seasons,

blade and byrnie, until his son could

noble deeds perform like his old father;

gave him then among Geats war-clothing

of all kinds, countless, when he from life went,

2625 wise, on way forth. Then was first time

for young warrior that he war's rush

with his noble lord engage should.

Not melted him the mood-heart, nor his father's legacy

艾尔佛的族人。

2605　他看见自己的国王
　　　头戴钢盔,被烈火团团围困,
　　　他没有忘记贝奥武甫赐予的恩惠,
　　　没有忘记他的领地威格蒙丁,以及
　　　他父亲所享有的种种权利。

2610　他这时毫不犹豫,一手紧握一面
　　　黄色椴木圆盾,一手拔出一把古剑。
　　　这把剑是欧赛尔之子伊恩蒙德
　　　留下的利器:当年威斯丹在战斗中
　　　杀死了无依无靠的流亡者,并把

2615　那闪亮的头盔、带环的胸甲,以及
　　　这把巨人制造的古剑带回族人中间,
　　　包括这柄锋利的宝剑,作为
　　　他的奖赏。他①后来闭口不谈这次杀戮,　　① 指奥尼拉。
　　　虽然死者是他兄弟的儿子。

2620　多年来,威斯丹一直佩带着
　　　这把宝剑,穿着这套盔甲,直到儿子
　　　长大成人,有能力和他一样建立功勋。
　　　在他弃世以前,他当着高特人的面
　　　把这套披挂和其他许多东西

2625　交到儿子手里。而此番出征
　　　对于这位年轻的武士,正是初次
　　　跟随可敬的主公出现在战场。
　　　他的勇气没有消退,双方

failed in fight;    that the serpent found

2630   when they together    tussled had.

Wiglaf spoke,    word-truths many

said to companions    —in him was heart sad—:

    "I that time recall,    where we mead received,

when we promised    to our lord

2635   in beer-hall,    who us these rings gave,

that we him the war-gear    repay would,

if for him just such    need arose,

helms and hard sword.    So he us from army chose

for this venture    of his own will,

2640   considered us worthy    and me these treasures gave,

because he us spear-fighters    good reckoned,

bold helm-bearers;    although lord for us

this courage-deed    alone intended

to achieve,    folk's keeper,

2645   because he of men most    glories achieved,

deeds daring.    Now is the day come

that our liege-lord    strength needs

of good warriors;    let us go to,

help battle-leader    while heat lasts,

2650   fire-terror fierce.    God knows of me

that me is much more welcome    that my body

with my gold-giver    fire embraces.

Not seems me right    that we shields bear

一经交锋,那火龙即刻发现自己

2630　奈何不了这柄祖传的宝剑。
　　　威格拉夫义正词严谴责他的伙伴,
　　　他的内心充满了无限的悲伤:
　　　"我记得有一回在宴乐厅喝酒,
　　　我们的主公赏给我们头盔和宝剑——

2635　他先前已赏给我们许多戒指与项圈——
　　　我们向他许过诺言,只要有什么危难
　　　降临到他身上,我们一定
　　　为他赴汤蹈火。他因此按自己的意愿
　　　从部属中挑选出我们参加这次历险。

2640　他以为我们值得享有这份荣耀——
　　　他还给了我许多金银财宝——
　　　他把我们当作真正的战士。
　　　尽管作为百姓的庇护人,他一心
　　　只想独自完成这英勇的壮举,

2645　因为他先前就曾创下人间奇迹。
　　　眼下正是我们的主公需要
　　　他的战士为他出力的时候。
　　　让我们前去与他会合,在这
　　　熊熊的烈焰中为我们的国王

2650　助上一臂之力。上帝作证,
　　　我宁可让熊熊的烈火吞食
　　　我的躯体,也要与恩主同在!
　　　如果我们不能打败仇敌,保护

back to home,　　unless we first may

2655　foe fell,　　life defend

of Wederas' chief.　　I know well

that were not past deeds such　　that he alone should

of Geats' retinue　　pain suffer,

sink in strife;　　for us shall sword and helm,

2660　byrnie and battle-shroud　　both together work."

　　　　Waded then through the death-smoke,　　war-helmet wore,

to lord's assistance,　　few words spoke:

　　　　"Dear Beowulf,　　do all well,

as you in youth-life　　long since said

2665　that you not would let,　　with you still living,

glory fail;　　you shall now, in deeds bold,

leader resolute,　　with all strength

life defend;　　I you will aid."

　　　　After those words　　serpent wrathful came,

2670　awful savage guest　　a second time

with fire-floods glowing　　foes to seek,

hated humans.　　Flame in waves flowed,

burned shield to boss,　　byrnie not could

to young spear-fighter　　protection provide,

2675　but the man young　　under his kinsman's shield

boldly went　　when his own was

by fire destroyed.　　Then again war-king

glories remembered,　　from main-strength struck

226

高特国王的性命,我们就无颜

2655　穿着戎装再见家乡父老!
　　　我知道,他过去建立过丰功伟绩,
　　　今天绝不该让他当着高特人的面
　　　单独忍受痛苦,葬身于火海。
　　　我要与他并肩作战,这份

2660　使刀弄剑的荣耀为我俩所共有!"
　　　他于是扑进致命的浓烟,头戴
　　　钢盔前去援助高特国王,他说:
　　　"亲爱的贝奥武甫,竭尽全力吧!
　　　你年轻时就曾说过,只要你

2665　一息尚存,就不能让荣誉丢失。
　　　坚强的主公,勇敢的战士,
　　　你现在必须奋力保护你自己,
　　　我威格拉夫将助你一臂之力!"
　　　话音刚落,那残忍而可怖的大蛇

2670　在火光中闪耀着躯体,怒气冲冲
　　　向它所仇视的勇士发起
　　　第二次进攻。大火弥漫整个洞府,
　　　坚盾烧得面目全非,胸甲无法
　　　为年轻的战士提供保护。

2675　当坚盾在火海中化为灰烬,
　　　他赶紧避进亲人的铁盾底下。
　　　这时,勇敢的国王再次想到
　　　自己的荣誉,他挥舞宝剑,

with battle blade     so that it in head stuck.

2680   by violence driven.    Nægling broke,

failed in fight    sword of Beowulf,

old and grey-lined.    To him it granted not was

that him irons'    edges might

help in battle;    was the hand so strong

2685   that blades all    —by my knowledge—

in stroke he over-strained,    when he to battle bore

weapon by wounds hardened;    was not him any the better.

Then was tribe-smasher    for third time,

fierce fire-dragon,    of feuds mindful,

2690   rushed at the brave king    when him chance allowed,

hot and battle-grim,    neck whole clamped

in fiendish fangs;    he drenched was

in soul-blood,    gore in waves gushed.


Then I at need heard    of folk-king

2695   alongside hero    courage showed,

strength and keenness    as in him native was.

Not heeded he the head,    though the hand was burned

of daring man,    as he his kinsman helped,

and he the hated foe    lower a little struck,

2700   man in armour,    so that the sword sank in

gleaming and golden,    so that the fire began

to slacken then.    Still himself king

使尽全部气力砍向毒龙的脑门。

2680　贝奥武甫的宝剑"尼格林"，

　　　这柄青灰的古剑断为两截，

　　　辜负了它的主人。利刃帮不上

　　　国王的忙，这也是命中注定。

　　　他的手太重，我曾听人说过，

2685　任何能置人于死地的利器

　　　一旦到了他的手里，都会被砍弯，

　　　刀枪剑戟对他全派不上用场。

　　　那百姓的屠夫，可怕的火龙，

　　　念念不忘自己的仇恨，觑准时机

2690　第三次向勇士发动进攻。

　　　它吐着火，用尖利的毒牙

　　　咬住国王的脖子，生命的鲜血

　　　喷涌而出，淋遍了国王的全身。


　　　然后，我听说，在这紧急关头，

2695　国王身边的勇士显示出他的勇敢、

　　　力量和机智——他的天赋。

　　　他避开龙头，尽管他的手

　　　在援助国王时已被烧伤，

　　　但他仍奋不顾身用剑刺向

2700　可恶的仇敌，宝剑金光闪闪，

　　　刺入毒龙的腰部，那火焰

　　　即刻熄灭。这时候国王

ruled his wits,     war-dagger drew,

bitter and battle-sharp,     that he on byrnie wore;

2705    sliced Wederas' leader     worm in middle.

Foe they felled     —courage drove out life—

and they him then both     battered had,

kin-nobles;     such should man be,

thane at need.     That for the chieftain was

2710    last victory-time     for his own deeds

in world of action.     Then the wound began,

which him the earth-dragon     earlier dealt,

to smart and swell;     he it soon found

that him in breast     with deadly rage welled

2715    poison within.     Then the hero went,

that he by wall     wise-thinking

sat on seat;     stared at giants' work,

how the stone arches     on pillars firm

timeless earth-house     inside held.

2720    Him then with hand,     sword-bloody

chief famous,     thane intensely good

friend-lord his     with water laved,

in battle sated,     and his helm unloosed.

Beowulf gave voice,     he over injury spoke,

2725    wound deadly;     knew he well

that he day-whiles     endured had,

earth's joy;     then was all dissolved

神志尚清,他从自己的盔甲上
拔出一把锋利无比的短剑,

2705　高特人的首领把毒龙一刀斩断。
他们终于杀死仇敌,勇气驱逐了
邪恶的生命,两位高贵的战士
联手把毒龙消灭。凡遇危难,
每个人都应如此。但对于贝奥武甫,

2710　这是他最后的一次胜利,
是他在这世上最后的壮举。
刚才毒龙造成的伤口已开始
发热、膨胀,他马上意识到
侵入胸口的毒素已经发作。

2715　善于思考的国王于是走到
悬崖边,找了个地方坐下。
他观看着这巨人创造的奇迹,
地下的宫廷内,那一根根石柱
如何牢牢地支撑起圆形屋顶。

2720　尤比仁义的勇士过来,用清水
给著名的国王清洗血污的伤口。
可敬的主公已经厌倦争战,
武士帮他摘下头上的钢盔。
贝奥武甫忍住剧烈的伤痛

2725　开口说话。他清楚地知道,
他已经享尽了人间的欢乐,
他在世的日子已到了尽头,

days' tally,　　death extremely near:

　　"Now I to son my　　give would

2730　war-garments,　　if me granted so

any heir　　after had been

to body belonging.　　I the nation ruled

fifty winters;　　was not the folk-king

of neighbours,　　any of them,

2735　who me with warriors　　approach dared,

with terror to oppress.　　I in land awaited

time's events,　　ruled my own well,

not sought treacheries,　　nor me swore any

oaths unjustly.　　I of it all may,

2740　with life-wounds sick,　　rejoicing have;

because me blame not need　　Ruler of men

for murder-death of kin,　　when my fades

life from body.　　Now you quickly go,

hoard examine　　under hoary stone,

2745　Wiglaf dear friend,　　now the serpent lies,

sleeps sorely wounded,　　of wealth bereft.

Be now in haste,　　so that I old riches,

gold-store, might see,　　keenly gaze at

shining skill-gems,　　so that I the easier may

2750　for treasure-wealth　　my leave

life and nation　　which I long ruled."

死神已一步步向他逼近：

"如果我死后有后代延续

2730　我的生命，此时，我应该

把这身盔甲传给我的儿子。

我治理这个国家已经有

五十个春秋；在这期间，

没有哪个邻邦的国王胆敢

2735　率兵侵犯我的国境，用恐怖威胁

我的子民。在自己的国土上，

我等待命运的安排，坚守

自己的家园，不谋阴险的争端，

不立虚假的誓言。尽管我此刻

2740　受了致命伤，但我心满意足，因为

当生命即将离开肉体之际，

万民的主不会对我横加指责，

说我残害了自己的亲人。

亲爱的威格拉夫，我的朋友，

2745　如今毒龙已受重创倒毙，

请你赶快去看看灰岩下的宝藏。

请一刻也不要迟疑，以便让我

亲眼看看那些古代的财宝，

亲眼见见那些奇异的珍玩，

2750　因为有了这笔财富，我可以

坦然地离开人生和自己的国土。"

Then I swiftly heard     son of Weohstan

after word-speech     wounded lord

obey, battle-sick king;     ring-mail wearing,

2755    braided battle-sark,     he went under barrow's roof.

Saw then victorious,     when he by seat went,

retainer resolute,     rich jewels many,

gold glittering     at ground level,

wonders on wall,     and the worm's den,

2760    old dawn-flier's,     cups standing,

former men's flagons,     burnishers gone,

ornaments stripped;     there was helm many

old and rusty,     arm-rings many

skilfully twisted.     Treasure easily may,

2765    gold in ground,     of mankind any one

overwhelm,     hide it he who will.

Also he hanging saw     standard all-golden

high over hoard,     of hand-wonders greatest,

linked with fingers' skill;     from it light stood,

2770    so that he the ground     make out might,

treasures examine.     Was not of the serpent there

sign any,     for him blade took.

Then I in mound heard     hoard rifle,

old giants' work,     one man,

2775    him in bosom load     bowls and plates

of self's choice;     standard also took,

我听说威斯丹之子当时没有怠慢，

即刻服从了受重伤的国王，

他遵照主公的嘱咐，身穿

2755　带环的盔甲进入了墓冢。

年轻的武士迈着胜利的步伐

越过毒龙的宝座，即刻看见

不计其数的财宝在龙窟，

在黑夜的飞行者的老巢

2760　闪闪发光。其中有各种金杯，

古人的饮具，因没有人擦拭，

装饰已经剥落。此外还有许多

锈迹斑斑的头盔、精巧的臂环。

这些地下的金银财宝早已

2765　把人类抛在它们的身后，不管

当初埋藏它的是士绅还是王侯。

武士还在这堆宝藏的上方

看见一面用金丝织成的战旗，

它巧夺天工，不愧为人间奇迹。

2770　那战旗还射出一道光芒，使他

能看清地上的财宝，只是大蛇

已无生息，它已丧命于剑下。

只身进入龙窟的武士，我听说，

就这样夺取了那堆宝藏，

2775　他心满意足，把那些金杯金盘

抱在怀里。他还取下那面

beacon brightest.     Blade already wounded

—edge was iron—     of ancient lord,

him who the treasures'     protector was

2780  for long while,     fire-terror waged

hot for hoard,     fiercely welling

at midnights     until he in slaughter died.

      Retainer was in haste,     for return eager,

by treasures urged on;     him curiosity drove

2785  whether, bold-hearted,     alive he would find

in the field-place,     Weder-Geats' chief,

strength-sick,     where he him earlier left.

He then with the treasures     glorious chief,

lord his own,     bleeding found,

2790  of life at end;     he him again began

with water to sprinkle,     until word's point

breast-hoard through-broke.     Warrior-king spoke,

old in grief,     gold he gazed at:

      "I for the riches     to Lord of all, thanks,

2795  to Glory-king,     in words say,

to eternal Lord,     which I here on stare,

that I was able     for my people

before death-day     such to store up.

Now I for treasures' hoard     with my have paid

2800  old allotted life,     you discharge from now on

nation's need;     not Can I here longer be.

光彩夺目的军旗,以及国王那把

锋利的宝剑,它曾重创过

那条大蛇。长年守护宝藏的卫士

2780　曾经趁黑夜打劫,喷吐恐怖之火

把宝库搅得热浪滚滚,直到

它一命呜呼,死于这场角逐。

威格拉夫取了这些财宝

急急回转;他心中十分焦虑,

2785　迫切想知道高特人的国王

气力衰竭后是否还活着,

是否仍待在刚才的地方。

武士带着财宝很快发现

他的主公,伟大的国王身上

2790　仍然在流血,生命已悬一线。

他赶紧又用水洒他,直到

他开口说话。勇敢的国王

心情沉重,看着那堆珠宝说:

"为了眼前这些玮宝明珠,

2795　我要感谢万能的主,光荣的王,

永恒的上帝,是他庇护我

在临终以前为自己的人民

获得这么巨大的一笔财富。

我用自己的残生换来这一切,

2800　你务必拿它去供养百姓。

我的生命已经十分有限,

Order war-famed men      mound to build,

bright after fire,      on ocean's cape;

it shall be reminder      to my people,

2805    high towering      on Hronesness,

so that it seafarers      then will call

Beowulf's barrow,      those who ships

over seas' shadows      from afar drive."

    Took him from neck      ring golden

2810    chief bold-minded,      to thane handed,

to young spear-fighter,      gold-bright helm,

ring and byrnie,      told him use them well:

    "You are last left      of our kin

of Wægmundings;      all fate lured

2815    my kinsmen      to destined death,

warriors in strength;      I them after must go."

    That was for the old man      final word

from breast-thoughts      before he pyre chose,

hot hostile flames;      him from heart went

2820    soul to seek      truly just men's glory.

请你在我火化后吩咐士兵，

让他们在海岸为我造一座墓。

以便我的人民前往悼念，

2805 这墓要高矗在赫罗斯尼斯山冈上，

这样，当航海者在茫茫的大海

驾驶他们高大的帆船航行，

就可称之为‘贝奥武甫之墓’。"

坚强的国王取下身上的项圈，

2810 金光闪闪的头盔、戒指和胸甲，

全都交给这个年轻的武士，

并关照他珍惜他的馈赠。

"你是我们威格蒙丁族最后一位武士；

命运席卷了我的全部宗亲，

2815 身强力壮的人都得告别人生，

我现在就将步他们的后尘。"

这就是老国王最后的肺腑之言，

不久葬礼的柴堆，可恨的火焰

将吞没他。他的灵魂将脱离肉体，

2820 踏上正直者归宿的旅程。

# PART TWELVE
## Beowulf's Funeral

Then was touched      man untried

painfully,     that he on ground saw

the dearest man    of life at end,

wretchedly suffering.    Slayer also lay,

2825    awesome earth-dragon,    of life bereft,

balefully beaten down.    Ring-hoard longer

serpent coiled    control not could,

but him irons'    edges took away,

hard, battle-sharp    hammers' leavings,

2830    so that the wide-flier,    by wounds stilled,

fell to floor,    hoard-cave near.

Not through air    flying turned

at midnights,    of rich possessions proud,

appearance showed,    but he on earth fell

2835    by the war-chief's    handwork.

Yet it on land    few men availed,

strength-owners,    to my knowledge,

though he in deeds all    daring were,

that he against poison-scourge's    breath rushed,

2840    or ring-hall    with hands disturbed,

# 十二
## 贝奥武甫的葬礼

年轻人悲痛万分,他看见
这世界上他最敬爱的人
在令人悲悯的痛苦中辞别人生。
凶手和他一样倒在地上,

2825 来自地狱的可怕毒龙丢了性命,
那是它罪有应得。盘曲的长虫
再也不能独占这些宝藏,
经过千锤百炼和战役磨砺的
宝剑锋刃,了结了它的性命。

2830 这飞行的怪兽一动不动,躺在
洞窟边的地上,它再也不能
深更半夜飞行在空中,扬扬得意于
自己的财产,显露自己的面目;
它如今已死,国王的双手

2835 结束了它的一生。据我所知,
世界上再找不到这样的勇士,
无论他是什么人,只要发现
居住在墓冢中的守护者
没有闭眼,依然能义无反顾,

2840 冒着有毒的火焰冲上前去,

241

if he watching    warder found

living in barrow.    For Beowulf was

noble treasures' share    with death repaid;

had each of them    at end arrived

2845    of loaned life.    Was not then long to when

the battle-slackers    forest left,

timid trust-breakers    ten together,

who not dared before    with spears to fight

in their liege-lord's    large need;

2850    but they, ashamed,    shields bore,

war-clothing,    to where the old man lay;

they looked at Wiglaf.    He wearied sat,

foot-fighter,    lord's shoulders near,

waked him with water;    him naught it helped.

2855    Not could he on earth,    though he wished well,

in the chieftain    life retain,

nor the Ruler's will    at all avert;

would decree of God    actions rule

of men all,    as he now still does.

2860    Then was from the young man    grim answer

easily obtained    for him who before his courage lost.

Wiglaf spoke,    Weohstan's son,

man sore at heart,    looked at unloved warriors:

"That indeed may say,    he who will truth speak,

2865    that the liege-lord    who you the treasures gave,

或者用他的双手把宝库

搅得天翻地覆。贝奥武甫

赢得了宝藏,却付出了生命。

在那租赁来的生命的旅程中,

2845　他和毒龙都已走到了尽头。

不久,那班临阵逃脱的武士

钻出树林,这十个背盟的懦夫

在主公危难的紧要关头

不敢手持武器挺身而出。

2850　这时他们满怀羞愧,全身披挂

来到老国王倒下的地方。

他们看着威格拉夫。勇士疲惫地

坐在主公身边,给他洒水,

想让他苏醒,但已无济于事。

2855　尽管他诚心诚意,但他无法

挽回国王的生命,主的旨意

丝毫不能变更。上帝的裁决

决定人间每一个人的命运,

就像他此刻裁决贝奥武甫。

2860　年轻的武士情不自禁,严厉指责

眼前这班缺乏勇气的士兵。

威斯丹之子心里好不凄楚,

两眼紧盯着这群可恨的懦夫:

"凡是诚实的人都会说,我们的主公

2865　曾经赏赐你们金银财宝,以及

war-trappings,    that you there in stand,

—when he on ale-bench    often handed

to hall-sitters    helm and byrnie,

chief to his thanes,    such as he grandest

2870    anywhere far or near    find could—

that he grossly    war-gear

woefully wasted,    when to him war came.

In no way folk-king    war comrades

to boast of needed;    yet to him God granted,

2875    victories' Ruler,    that he himself avenged

alone with sword,    when for him was valour's need.

    I him life-protection    little could

give in fight,    and began however

beyond my strength-measure    kinsman to help;

2880    ever was the weaker    when I with sword struck

deadly enemy;    fire less fiercely

welled from head.    Defenders too few

thronged round chieftain    when for him the crisis came.

Now shall treasure-getting    and sword-giving,

2885    all homeland-joy    for your kin,

comfort, cease;    of land-right must

of your kin-clan    man every

deprived become,    when nobles

from afar learn    of flight your,

2890    inglorious deed.    Death is better

你们手上的这些作战武器。

他还常常在宴乐厅向赴宴者

分发头盔和盔甲，那都是

普天之下最珍贵的礼品，然而，

2870　在争战降临他身上的时候，

这一切算是白白给扔了！

你们的行为真让人痛心！

高特人的国王没有必要吹嘘

手下的战士。是上帝，胜利的统帅

2875　在他需要勇气时援助了他，

使他单枪匹马向仇敌讨还血债。

在激战中，我未能保护住

他的生命，但我已竭尽全力

帮助了我的亲人。凶残的仇敌

2880　被我的剑刺中，它的威力

逐渐消退，它喷吐的火焰

很快减弱。可惜在紧急关头，

国王身边除了我没有一个救兵。

从今以后，再不会有人向你们

2885　赏赐珠宝，赠送宝剑和战刀。

安居乐业的日子从此一去不返。

当四方贵族知道你们临阵逃脱，

犯下可耻的罪过，你们的家族

必将被剥夺所拥有的一切特权。

2890　对于一个战士来说，与其

for men all      than shame-life."


     Commanded then the battle-deed      in camp announced

up over edge-cliff,      where the warrior-band

morning-long day      sad-hearted sat,

2895  shield-bearers,      either expecting

death-day      or return

of dear man.      Little withheld

of new tidings      he who headland rode,

but he truly      said before all:

2900      "Now is joy-giver      of Wederas' nation

lord of Geats      on deathbed still,

lies in slaughter-rest      from serpent's deeds;

him beside lies      his life-taker,

with dagger-wounds sick;      with sword not might he

2905  on the monster      in any way

wounds inflict.      Wiglaf sits

over Beowulf,      son of Weohstan,

one hero over other      unliving,

holds heart-weary      head—watch

2910  over loved and loathed.      Now is for nation likely

warfare-time      when revealed

to Franks and Frisians      fall of king

widely becomes.      Was the quarrel shaped

fierce against Franks,      when Hygelac came

活着被人唾骂,不如一死谢罪!"

　　然后他发布命令,将战报传回城堡,
　　成群的武士在悬崖上坐了一上午,
　　他们手持坚盾,心情沉重,
2895　急切想知道他们敬爱的人
　　是否活着,能否平安无事地
　　返回宫廷。信使向来诚实,
　　当他骑着快马翻过海岬,
　　便如实把发生的事转告大家:
2900　"高特人的主公,欢乐的赐予者,
　　已经驾崩升遐;他被毒龙所伤,
　　倒在凶手的巢穴。在他身边
　　躺着他的死敌,毒龙的身上
　　留着短剑的创伤。任何刀枪
2905　本来不能给那怪物造成伤害。
　　威斯丹之子威格拉夫坐在
　　贝奥武甫身旁,活着的英雄
　　面对死去的英雄,守灵人
　　已心力交瘁,身边躺着两具尸体:
2910　一具令人可敬,一具令人可憎。
　　国王倒下了,死讯一旦传到
　　法兰克人和弗罗西亚人耳里,
　　我们的民族就将面临一场战争。
　　当年海格拉克率领军队

2915    faring with sea-force      into Frisians' land;

there him the Hetware      in battle attacked,

with courage caused,      with over-strength,

that the mailed warrior      bow down must,

fell among foot-troop;      no riches gave

2920    lord to retinue.      For us was ever after

the Merovingian king's      mercy ungranted.

Not I from Swedes' tribe      peace or trust

at all expect,      for was widely known

that Ongentheow      of life deprived

2925    Hæthcyn Hrethel's son      at Ravenswood,

when for arrogance      first attacked

Geats' nation      War-Scylfings.

At once him the wise      father of Ohthere,

old and awesome,      onslaught returned,

2930    cut down sea-leader,      wife rescued,

ancient old woman,      of gold bereft,

Onela's mother      and Ohthere's;

and then pursued      life-enemies

until they escaped      uneasily

2935    into Ravensholt      without a lord.

He besieged then with vast army      swords' refugees

with wounds weary;      woe often vowed

to wretched band      in endlong night,

said he in morning      with sword's edges

2915　进入弗罗西亚领土,结果

　　　　与法兰克人发生激烈的争战,

　　　　海特威尔人①以优势的兵力　　　　　① 法兰克部落
　　　　　　　　　　　　　　　　　　　　　之一。
　　　　向他进攻,很快使披甲的武士

　　　　招架不住,倒在士兵之中。

2920　他没有财宝赏赐他的扈从,

　　　　而墨洛温王的友谊却从此断送。

　　　　同样,瑞典人的和平与信任

　　　　我也不敢奢望。众所周知,

　　　　奥根索在莱芬窝德附近

2925　杀了赫斯辛,雷塞尔的儿子。

　　　　当时的高特人趾高气扬,

　　　　首先向善战的瑞典人宣战。

　　　　欧赛尔的父亲②老奸巨猾,　　　　② 指奥根索。

　　　　率领军兵反攻,结果砍了

2930　海上之王③的头颅,救了他的妻子,　③ 指赫斯辛。

　　　　那位被剥夺财产的王后,

　　　　奥尼拉和欧赛尔的母亲。

　　　　他后来还穷追不舍,一直

　　　　把失去领袖的仇敌赶到

2935　莱芬窝德。他指挥他的军兵

　　　　把一班残兵败将团团围困,

　　　　一遍遍发誓要让这些不幸的人

　　　　痛苦地熬上一夜,并声称次日一早,

　　　　他要用宝剑砍下他们的脑袋,

2940  slaughter would,      some on gallows-trees

for birds' delight.      Relief back came

to anguished-minds      with early day

when they Hygelac's      horn and trumpet

sounding heard,      then the good king came

2945  with tribe's retainers      on track faring.


Was the blood-swathe      of Swedes and Geats,

death-clash of men,      widely seen,

how the folk between them      feud upstirred.

Went then the good king      with his companions,

2950  wise, very sad,      fortress to seek,

earl Ongentheow      farther retreated,

had of Hygelac's      battle-skill heard,

proud king's war-craft;      resistance not trusted,

that he sea-men      withstand could,

2955  against war-sailors      hoard defend,

children and women;      drew back thence

old behind earth-wall.      Then was chase offered

to Swedish nation,      standards of Hygelac

refuge-place that      forth overran,

2960  when Hrethel's heirs      to garrison thronged.

There was Ongentheow      by edges of swords,

grizzle-haired,      to bay brought,

so that the tribe-king      submit must

2940 然后挂上绞刑架,任凭鸟儿
美美地享用。然而,天一亮,
心情沮丧的人又有了希望,
他们听见海格拉克吹响号角,
仁义的国王亲率一支大军
2945 前来救援,出现在大道上。


于是,瑞典人和高特人展开
一场大战,直杀得血流成河,
两个民族的仇恨就此继续加深。
仁义的国王然后带着族人
2950 无比悲痛地撤回他的城堡,
奥根索则比他撤得更远,因为
他早就听说海格拉克骁勇善战,
斗志高昂。他不敢继续抵抗,
不相信自己有能力打败
2955 好水性的高特人,保住自己的财产、
妻子和儿女。因此他没有进攻,
反而后撤,躲进了土墙背后。
接着轮到瑞典人被人追击,
雷塞尔的人马向前步步逼近,
2960 海格拉克的战旗在敌营飘扬。
白发苍苍的奥根索被宝剑
逼上绝路,这位部落的首领
把自己的命运交给奥佛尔

to Eofor's sole judgement.     Him angrily
2965   Wulf, Wonred's son,     with weapon cut,
so that from him by blow     blood in streams sprang
forth under hair.     Not was he afraid however,
aged Scylfing,     but repaid fast
with deadlier riposte     death-blow that,
2970   when tribe-king     thither turned.
Not could the brave     son of Wonred
to old man     onslaught give,
for Ongentheow him on head     helm had sheared,
so that Wulf, blood-stained,     bow down must,
2975   fell to ground;     not was he doomed yet,
but he recovered,     though him wound hurt.
Caused the hard     Hygelac's thane, Eofor,
broad blade,     when his brother lay,
old-sword ogreish,     giant helm
2980   to break over shield-wall;     then bowed king,
folk's keeper,     was fatally hit.
Then were many     who Eofor's kinsman bandaged,
quickly raised him     when for them room cleared was,
so that they slaughter-place     to win were able.
2985   Then stripped     one man the other,
took from Ongentheow     iron byrnie,
hard sword hilted     and his helmet too;
hoary king's armour     to Hygelac bore.

一人裁决。华莱德之子奥尔夫
2965　怒气冲天，用宝剑先刺中了他，
　　　殷红的血从他的发际上
　　　喷涌而出。年迈的瑞典国王
　　　毫不畏惧，他即刻转过身来，
　　　用剑还击奥尔夫。他的一剑
2970　更其凶狠，足以置人于死地。
　　　勇敢的华莱德之子未能
　　　再向老人进攻，因为奥根索
　　　已经先把他的头盔砍穿，使得
　　　奥尔夫血流满面，扑倒在地。
2975　但他命不该绝，他的伤势
　　　虽然严重，但他仍然活着。
　　　海格拉克的勇士奥佛尔看见
　　　自己的兄弟倒在地上，即刻拔出
　　　他的宝剑，那把巨人铸造的利刃，
2980　砍穿老王的坚盾，刺破他的头盔。
　　　老王终于倒下，阵亡在战场。
　　　许多高特人过来为奥佛尔的兄弟
　　　包扎伤口，很快把他扶起。至此，
　　　他们已经主宰整个战场。
2985　奥佛尔从死者身上剥下武装——
　　　他脱下奥根索的胸甲，并摘下
　　　他的宝剑和头盔。他把战利品
　　　全都交给国王海格拉克。

He the treasures took    and him fairly pledged

2990   rewards among tribe,    and made good so;

paid for the war-clash    Geats' lord,

Hrethel's heir,    when he home returned,

Eofor and Wulf    with much treasure,

gave them both    a hundred thousand worth

2995   of land and linked rings;    not needed him the gifts reproach

any man on middle-earth,    since they the glories gained in war;

and then to Eofor he gave    his only daughter,

home-honouring,    as favour's pledge.

    That is the feud    and the enmity,

3000   death-hate of men,    for which I expect

that us attack    Swedes' nation

when they learn    leader our

gone from life,    he who formerly guarded

against haters    hoard and kingdom,

3005   after heroes' fall    keen shield-fighters,

folk-good upheld,    or further yet

fine deeds performed.    Now is haste best,

that we tribe-king    there look upon,

and the one bring,    who us rings gave,

3010   on pyre-journey.    Not shall mere pittance

melt with the mighty king,    but there is treasures' hoard,

gold uncounted,    grimly purchased,

and now at last    with own life

国王收下这份厚礼,答应给他

2990　重重嘉奖,这话他说到做到。
　　　回国以后,高特人的国王、
　　　雷塞尔的继承人,赏了两兄弟
　　　许多金银财宝,还赐给每人
　　　价值可观的领地和一些项圈。

2995　兄弟俩战功卓著,世人没有理由
　　　对他们所得的奖赏说三道四。
　　　作为恩宠的见证,国王还把独生女
　　　嫁给奥佛尔,使他门第生辉。
　　　这就是两国间的宿怨和敌意,

3000　不共戴天的仇恨。我可以预料
　　　瑞典人一定会进攻我们,一旦
　　　他们得知我们的国王已经仙逝。
　　　先前是他保护我们的家园和财产
　　　免遭仇人的蹂躏与掠夺,自从

3005　几位英雄①陨落,是他保护了
　　　百姓的利益,做了许许多多
　　　善事嘉行。现在马上出发吧,
　　　让我们这就去看看我们的国王,
　　　把赏赐我们项圈的恩主抬上

3010　火葬的柴堆。伟人的陪葬
　　　不可太吝啬,应有整个宝库,
　　　无数的黄金;他以生命的代价
　　　换来的一切都得随他一起火化,

① 指海格拉克
兄弟。

255

rings he bought; then shall blaze devour,

3015 flame enfold. No man shall wear

these treasures in his memory, no woman fair

have on neck ring-ornament,

but shall sad-hearted, gold-bereft,

often, not once, alien-land tread,

3020 now the war-leader laughter has laid aside,

pleasure and merriment. Therefore shall spear be

many morning-cold in fingers grasped,

raised in hands; not harp's clang

warrior wakes, but the black raven

3025 eager for doomed men, much screeching,

to eagle telling how he at eating fared

when he with wolf the slain despoiled."

 So the man bold teller was

of hateful tidings; he not lied much

3030 in deeds or words. Troop all arose,

went unhappy under Earnaness

with welling tears the wonder to gaze at.

Found then on sand, soulless,

death-bed keeping, he who them rings gave

3035 in former times; then was end-day

for good man come, that the war-king,

Wederas' chieftain, wonder-death died.

 First they there saw stranger creature,

让烈焰把那些财宝吞噬殆尽。

3015  任何人都不得保留这些财宝。
　　　作为纪念,任何漂亮的女人
　　　都不可把项圈戴上自己的脖子。
　　　既然英雄的主公已经弃绝
　　　人间的幸福与欢乐,他的子民

3020  别想再活得快活,他们将一个个
　　　离乡背井。不管天气多么寒冷,
　　　他们一大早就得把长矛紧握在手。
　　　唤醒武士的声音不再是
　　　清越的竖琴,而是乌鸦的聒噪。

3025  它们在气数已尽的人身边低飞,
　　　向老鹰叙述它们的经历,
　　　夸耀自己如何与狼争食尸体。"
　　　就这样,勇敢的使者报告了
　　　可怕的消息;他的预言将会应验。

3030  所有的人都应声而起,他们
　　　一个个泪流满面,悲伤地赶往
　　　厄纳斯①观看这奇异的景象。

　　　① 地名,贝奥
武甫屠龙之地。

　　　他们很快发现,先前分赐项圈的人
　　　躺在沙地上,他的灵魂已经

3035  脱离躯体。仁慈而勇敢的国王,
　　　高特人的首领,已经走完
　　　人生的旅程,他死得壮烈!
　　　他们还看见那怪物的尸体

serpent on ground     opposite there

3040     loathed lying;     was the fire-dragon

gruesomely grim-hued,     by flames scorched;

it was fifty     foot—measures

long as it lay;     in air—joy ruled

at night a while,     down again went

3045     den to seek;     was then in death fixed,

had of earth-caves     its end enjoyed.

Him by stood     cups and flagons,

plates lay     and precious swords

by rust through-eaten,     as if they in earth's clasp

3050     thousand winters     there remained;

then was that legacy     of mighty power,

former men's gold,     with spell surrounded,

so that the ring-hall     touch not might

men any,     unless God himself,

3055     victories' true-King,     allowed whom he would

—he is men's protector—     hoard to open,

even so to each of men     as Him fitting seemed.


Then was seen     that the act not prospered

him who unrightly     inside had hidden

3060     jewels under wall.     Warden first slew

of few one man;     then the feud was

avenged angrily.     It is a wonder where then

就躺在国王对面,那模样

3040 真令人恶心。火龙的身躯
被火烧得光怪陆离,十分吓人。
它的身长足足有五十英尺。
它曾经自由自在飞行在夜空,
回来后就钻入栖身的墓冢。

3045 如今死亡已使它变得僵硬,
从此再进不了它的地洞。
它的身边堆着金杯金盘,
被铁锈腐蚀的宝刀宝剑,
这一切在大地的怀抱里

3050 不知沉睡了多少个春夏秋冬。
这笔巨大的遗产,古人的黄金,
已被符咒镇住,因此,任何人
都不得靠近藏宝的大殿,
除非上帝自己,那胜利之王,

3055 人类的保护者,允许某个人
打开这个宝库,无论是谁,
首先得讨得上帝的欢喜。


我们已经看到,那个私自
窝藏财宝的怪物没有捞到

3060 半点好处。它首先害死一位
杰出的人物,然后这笔血债
被如数讨还。这真是件奇事,

259

hero courage-famed     end shall meet

of destined life,     when longer not may

3065    man with his kinfolk     mead-hall inhabit.

So it was for Beowulf     when he barrow's guardian

sought, fierce combats;     self not knew

through what his world's departing     caused should be.

So it until doom's day     deeply cursed,

3070    chieftains glorious     who it there put,

so that the man would be     of sins guilty,

in shrines imprisoned,     in hell-bonds firm,

by evils punished,     who the place plundered;

not he gold-rich     too eagerly had

3075    owner's legacy     earlier examined.

Wiglaf spoke,     Weohstan's son:

"Often shall men many,     through one's will,

anguish suffer,     as to us has happened.

Not could we lend     loved chieftain,

3080    kingdom's keeper,     advice any,

that he not confront     gold-guard the,

let him lie     where he long was,

haunts occupy     until world's end;

he held to high destiny.     Hoard is exposed,

3085    grimly gained;     was the fate too harsh

which the tribe-king     thither drove.

I was there, inside,     and it all examined,

一位以勇力著称的贵胄竟然

就此丧生,再不能与亲人一道

3065 　居住在欢饮蜜酒的大厅里。

墓冢的卫士就这样与贝奥武甫

发生争战。当时他并不知道

自己将如何离开这个世界。

古代的王公埋藏财宝的当初

3070 　就已下过一道沉重的符咒:

在末日审判以前,任何人侵犯此地

都罪孽深重,必将囚禁于

邪教的庙堂,被地狱之索捆绑,

受恶魔的摧残,除非主的恩宠

3075 　首先降临在取宝人的身上。

威斯丹之子威格拉夫说:

"一人之死常常令万人蒙难,

这样的事今天就发生在我们身上。

我们未能劝说敬爱的主公,

3080 　王国的庇护人不去靠近

那黄金的卫士,任凭毒龙

一如既往待在自己的巢穴,

自由出没,直到世界末日。

他偏要认命。如今宝藏已打开,

3085 　但代价太惨重。百姓的恩主

被强大的命运驱使到这里。

道路一旦扫清,我也曾进入龙窟,

room's treasures,     when for me way cleared was;

not at all gently was     entry allowed

3090   in under earth-wall.     I in haste seized

huge, with hands,     vast burden

of hoarded wealth,     here out carried

to king my.     Alive he was then still,

alert and aware;     many things said

3095   old man in grief,     and you to greet told me,

bade that you build     for friend's deeds

in pyre-spot     barrow the high,

great and glorious,     as he of men was

warrior worthiest     widely through earth,

3100   while he fort-wealth     to enjoy was able.

Let us now hasten     another time,

see and seek     skill-gems' heap,

wonder under wall;     I you will guide

so that you enough     near-to gaze on

3105   rings and broad gold.     Let be the barrow ready,

quickly built,     when we out come,

and then carry     lord our,

loved man,     where he long must

in the Ruler's     keeping stay."

3110   Told then to order     son of Weohstan,

hero battle-brave,     warriors many,

homestead owners,     that they pyre-wood

亲眼看见一洞府的金银财宝。
对我而言,这次墓冢之行充满
3090 百般风险。当时我匆匆忙忙
用双手捧了许多金银珠宝
回到这里献给我的国王。
他当时还活着,神志尚清,
悲痛中,老人说了许多话,
3095 嘱咐我把大家召集起来。
在举行火葬的地方,为了纪念
主公的丰功伟绩,我们要为他
建造一座高大的坟墓,因为
在他享受城堡荣华的日子里,
3100 他是人世间最伟大的武士。
现在让我们马上再去看看
悬崖内那一大堆金银财宝,
我在前面为你们带路,以便
大家把许多项圈与黄金
3105 看个清楚。柴堆要即刻准备停当,
一等我们从毒龙的宝窟返回,
大家就动手把我们的国王,
可敬的主公抬起,让他永远
在主的庇护下长眠、安息。”
3110 威斯丹之子,战场上的英雄
于是发布命令,责成众武士,
厅堂的拥有者,百姓的首领,

from far fetched,      folk-leaders,

to good man's presence:      "Now shall fire consume,

3115    grown dark the flame,      warriors' ruler,

he who often braved      iron-shower

when arrows' storm      by strings impelled

shot over shield-wall,      shaft to task held,

in feather-gear eager,      arrow-head followed."

3120    But the wise      son of Weohstan

chose from the core      of king's thanes

seven together,      the finest;

he went, of eight one,      under enemy roof,

of battle-warriors;      one in hands bore

3125    fire-light,      he who in front walked.

Not was then lot-drawing      for who the hoard plundered

when unguarded      any part

men saw      in hall remaining,

useless lying;      little anyone lamented

3130    that they quickly      out carried

precious treasures;      dragon too they shoved,

serpent over wall-cliff,      let wave take,

flood enfold      jewels' keeper.

Then was wound gold      on wagon laden,

3135    of all kinds, countless,      and the king carried,

hoary battle-warrior,      to Hronesness.

到各处搜集木柴,为仁慈的国王
准备葬礼。他说:"浓烟滚滚的大火
3115 不久就要吞噬武士的统帅。
想当年,他常常出生入死,
冒着枪林箭雨冲锋陷阵,
带羽毛的箭镞满天横飞,
射穿坚盾威胁他的性命。"

3120 英明的威斯丹之子于是
从国王的扈从中挑选出
七名最优秀的战士,连他自己
一共八人,一道进入悬崖峭壁。
其中一人手中举着火把

3125 走在队伍前面。他们无须抽签
决定由谁负责夺取宝藏,因为
大家看见,洞府里一片萧然,
没有任何严阵以待的卫士。
当他们迅速搬出金银财宝,

3130 更没有人为之扼腕叹息。
他们还把毒龙拖出,推下
海边悬崖,让汹涌的海浪
把这珠宝的卫士吞没。然后,
他们把不计其数的黄金

3135 连同国王的尸体载上马车,
一起运到赫罗斯尼斯附近。

For him then made ready　　　Geats' people

pyre on earth,　　unpaltry,

with helmets hung,　　with battle-shields,

3140　with bright byrnies　　as he bidding was;

laid then in midst　　famed chieftain

heroes lamenting,　　lord beloved.

Began then on barrow　　bale-fire greatest

warriors to kindle;　　wood-smoke arose

3145　black above blaze,　　soughing flame

with Weeping woven　　—wind-blend allayed—

until it the bone-house　　broken had

hot at heart.　　In thought unhappy,

mind-care they moaned,　　liege-lord's death;

3150　so too grief-song　　Geatish woman

for Beowulf,　　bound-haired,

sang sorrow-caring,　　said anew

that she for herself harm-days　　harsh dreaded,

slaughters many,　　troop's terror,

3155　torture and captivity.　　Heaven smoke swallowed.

　　Wrought then　　Wederas' people

shelter on headland,　　it was high and broad,

for wave-farers　　widely visible,

and they built　　in ten days

3160　battle-chief's beacon,　　burning's remains

with wall encircled,　　as it most worthily

然后,高特人遵照国王的遗愿

为他的葬礼架起一座柴堆,

高大无比,那上面还挂着

3140 头盔、圆盾和闪亮的胸甲。

他们失声痛哭,在柴堆正中

放下伟大的国王,敬爱的英雄。

武士们在山冈上把葬礼的火点燃,

乌黑的浓烟在火舌上升腾,

3145 熊熊的大火怒吼着,与哭泣声

交杂在一起。风势逐渐减弱,

直到大火分解尸骨,柴堆中心

一片通红。人们心情沉重,

为国王的死表示深切哀悼。

3150 一位束发老妇为贝奥武甫唱起

凄凉的歌曲,一遍又一遍哭诉

她的忧虑,担心敌人的侵犯、

无数的杀戮、战争的恐怖、

对百姓的凌辱和掳掠即将来临。

3155 滚滚的浓烟此时已消失在天际。

高特人然后在海岬上动工修建

一座又高又大的陵墓,航海者

从老远的地方就能看见。

它成了英雄的纪念碑,整个工程

3160 十天之内完工,石墙内安放着

武士的骨灰。如此雄伟的陵墓

the cleverest men        construct might.

They in barrow placed        rings and brooches,

all such trappings        as from hoard before

3165    hostile-minded men        removed had;

they let heroes' treasure        earth hold,

gold in grit,        where it now still lives,

for men as useless        as it earlier was.

        Then around mound rode        battle-brave men,

3170    nobles' sons,        in all twelve;

wished sorrow to lament        and king to mourn,

word-song work out        and about man speak;

they praised heroic acts        and his courage-deeds,

excellence exalted,        as it fitting is

3175    that man his friend-lord        in words honours,

in heart loves,        when he forth must

from body-covering        led be.

Thus lamented        Geats' people

lord's fall,        heath-companions;

3180    said that he was        of world-kings,

of men, mildest        and most gentle,

to nation kindest,        and most keen for fame.


( *Fin.* )

只有最杰出的工匠才能建造。

他们还把许多项圈和珠宝

放进墓室,不安的人们从龙窟

3165　所获取的一切都成了国王的陪葬。

他们让古人的财富重新回到

大地的怀抱。这笔宝藏至今还在,

过去于人无用,今天依然无益。

十二位男士,贵族的子弟,

3170　骑马绕着坟墓走了几圈。

他们以此向国王致哀,口中

唱着挽歌,一遍遍叨念英雄。

他们赞美他的丰功伟绩,

他的勇气和神力。我们人类

3175　应该用语言尊崇自己的明主,

应该用全心挚爱自己的首领,

一旦他抛弃肉体,离开人间。

高特国的百姓、国王的亲信

也就这样悼念自己的主公。

3180　他们都说世上所有的国王

数他最仁慈、最温和、最善良,

最渴望为自己争取荣光。

(全文完)

269

# APPENDIX  Personal Name List
## 附录：人名表
（以中文译文出场顺序排列）

斯基夫（Scef），丹麦王希尔行之父。

希尔德（Scyld），丹麦王，贝奥之父。

贝奥（Beow），丹麦王，希尔德之子。

哈夫丹（Halfdane），贝奥之子，赫罗斯加之父。

希罗加（Heorogar），贝奥之子，赫加斯加之兄。

赫罗斯加（Hrothgar），丹麦王，鹿厅的建造者。

哈尔格（Halga），赫罗斯加之弟。

伊丝（Yrse），赫罗斯加之妹。

奥尼拉（Onela），瑞典王奥根索之子，娶伊丝之妻。


一

格兰道尔（Grendel），袭击鹿厅的恶魔，诗人称之为该隐的后裔。


二

海格拉克（Hygelac），高特王，贝奥武甫的舅父。

贝奥武甫（Beowulf），史诗主人公，高特武士，后来成为高特国王。

艾克塞奥（Ecgtheow），贝奥武甫之父。

乌夫加（Wulfgar），温德尔人的酋长，鹿厅的传令官。

雷塞尔（Hrethel），高特王，贝奥武甫的外公。

希塞拉夫(Heatholaf),威尔芬部落武士,为贝奥武甫之父艾克塞奥所杀。

### 三

安佛斯(Unferth),丹麦武士,艾格拉夫之子。

艾格拉夫(Ecglaf),丹麦武士。

布雷克(Breca),布朗丁部落武士,比斯丹之子,少年时曾与贝奥武甫
　　在大海中比赛游泳。

维瑟欧(Wealhtheow),赫罗斯加的王后。

### 五

西格蒙德(Sigmund),传说中的英雄,曾杀死过毒龙。

威尔斯(Wæls),西格蒙德的父亲。

菲特拉(Fitela),西格蒙德的外甥。

海勒摩德(Heremod),传说中的丹麦暴君。

赫罗索夫(Hrothulf),丹麦王赫罗斯加的侄子。

英格(Ing),传说中的丹麦国王。

芬恩(Finn),朱特部落酋长。

赫纳夫(Hnæf),丹麦部落酋长。

希德贝尔(Hildeburh),丹麦王霍克之女,赫纳夫的姐姐,芬恩之妻。

霍克(Hoc),传说中的丹麦王。

亨格斯特(Hengest),赫纳夫手下将领,史诗残片《芬斯堡之战》的
　　主角。

福克华尔德(Folcwalda),芬恩之父。

亨拉夫(Hunlaf),赫纳夫手下将领,死于朱特人之手。

古德拉夫(Gudlaf),亨拉夫的兄弟。

奥斯拉夫(Oslaf)，享拉夫的兄弟。

赫里斯雷克(Hrethric)，丹麦王赫罗斯加之子。

赫里斯雷德(Hrothmund)，丹麦王赫罗斯加之子。

爱曼里克(Eormenric)，东哥特王国国王。

斯华丁(Swerting)，高特老王，海格拉克之祖父。

六

叶曼拉夫(Yrmenlaf)，赫罗斯加的侍臣。

伊斯切尔(Æschere)，叶曼拉夫之兄，赫罗斯加的亲信，被格兰道尔的
    母亲所害。

八

艾克瓦拉(Ecgwela)，丹麦早期国王。

九

希格德(Hygd)，赫罗斯加的王后。

海勒斯(Hæreth)，希格德之父。

莫德莱丝(Modthryth)，恶公主的典型，后来嫁麦西亚国王奥法。

海敏(Hemming)，麦西亚早期国王。

奥法(Offa)，麦西亚国王，娶莫德莱丝为妻。

奥玛尔(Eomer)，麦西亚国王奥法之子。

加蒙德(Garmund)，奥法之父。

奥根索(Ongentheow)，瑞典人的国王，死于海格拉克讨伐瑞典的战斗中。

弗莱瓦鲁(Frearwaru)，赫罗斯加的女儿。

英格德(Ingeld)，希索巴人的国王弗罗达之子，后聚弗莱瓦鲁为妻。

272

弗罗达(Froda),希索巴部落酋长。

威塞哥尔德(Withergyld),希索巴部落武士。

汉德修(Hondscio),赫罗斯加手下武士,为格兰道尔所害。

希罗窝德(Heoroweard),赫罗斯加的侄儿,其兄希史加之子。

## 十

赫德莱德(Heardred),海格拉克之子,其父死后继承王位。

赫莱里克(Hereric),王后希格德的兄弟。

欧赛尔(Ohthere),瑞典国王奥根索的儿子,奥尼拉的兄弟,其父死后
    继承王位。

伊吉尔斯(Eadgils),欧赛尔之子,后来在贝奥武甫的援助下杀死篡位
    的叔父奥尼拉,成为瑞典的国王。

赫巴德(Herebeald),高特国王海格拉克的长兄,被其弟赫斯辛误伤而亡。

赫斯辛(Hæthcyn),高特国王海格拉克的兄弟,为奥根索所杀。

奥佛尔(Eofor),高特武士,瑞典国王奥根索即被他所杀。

达莱芬(Dæghrefn),法兰克部落武士,为贝奥武甫所杀。

## 十一

威斯丹(Weohstan),高特武士,威格拉夫之父。

威格拉夫(Wiglaf),助贝奥武甫杀死毒龙的高特武士。

伊恩蒙德(Eanmund),瑞典国王欧赛尔之子,被威格拉夫之父威斯丹所杀。

## 十二

华莱德(Wonred),高特武士,奥佛尔和奥尔夫之父。

奥尔夫(Wulf),高特武士,奥佛尔的兄弟。